DURINGWITCH

Piccadilly Circus in the rush hour. Neither Dr Oona Charrington nor her husband, Mycroft, a research scientist, notice the newspaper headlines which read ULTIMATUM: but suddenly officials, explaining there is an emergency, direct them to lifts. They are carried down, unknowingly, into a world of a totally new zoology and a landscape of great beauty which induces an intoxicating peace of mind.

They meet Berenice, a painter, and Nicholas, a monk, and all four are brought into a house where nothing is wanting and which resembles a piece of the finest blown glass. But why are they here?

DURINGWITCH

Keith Claire

EYRE & SPOTTISWOODE · LONDON

S.B.N. 413 44330 2

First published 1968
Copyright © Keith Claire
Printed in Great Britain by
Cox & Wyman Ltd.,
Fakenham, Norfolk

From London to York and Edinburgh the Furnaces rage
  terrible.
Primrose Hill is the mouth of the Furnace and the Iron
  Door.

William Blake, Jerusalem

I

Piccadilly Circus . . .

Money falling in machines.

The clatter of coins tumbling into up-ended and illuminated coffins. Crowds giving coins and receiving cardboard. Insects about their rituals, come unrecognized, perform their necessary act and then go down.

People go down. Money falling in machines.

Machines carrying people down.

Oona Charrington has a grim inner smile for the pathetic brilliance of the advertisers. And her husband fumbles for the tickets. Tall, a little shambling in a shabby overcoat, shabby because so many other things are so interesting. Doctor Oona enjoys waiting for him. He has talents that other people are afraid of, he has a laboratory where he watches disease flourish, where he cultivates plagues like flowers (for microbes can be curiously beautiful), where he watches his piebald mice lie still and die. Thousands of mice are dying while millions of bacilli grow strong, divide, multiply, go their ways and develop into something new. Mice breed, little bundles of trembling white and pink fur, trembling together.

Bacilli may have a right to life.

Mycroft Charrington precisely watching the activity in his laboratory of glass, contriving his epidemics, his computer thinking under his hand. Mice in his hand, delicate membranes, ears and whiskers, pink noses snifferting. In his world many mice die that a man may live, but this does not mean that Mycroft has no affection for his little creatures.

Sometimes he fills his pipe with his Gold Block tobacco and contemplates many mice scurrying under transparent domes and through small passages of glass. Mice go down. Mice go scurrying down.

Yet still he remembers, he has always remembered, to purchase the tickets in advance. Mycroft Charrington with the narrow face under the high shock of fading hair, ticket hunting, people swaying round him, Piccadilly. But he is himself.

Doctor Oona Charrington stands still and is the cut of her suit. To be aware of the suit is to know the quality of one's presence – patients feel confidence – male patients enjoy their diseases. The piled black hair that can be let down. (She must remember to telephone the hospital when they get back.)

Mycroft's slow, slightly halting smile. The hand that still reaches out for hers, she does not often hold his arm. She holds the long hand. The tickets are with him.

'The Piccadilly Line,' he says almost diffidently, though knowing so exactly where they are going and how they are going. Home, their house, South Kensington, number thirty-four, destination familiar.

They go forward to go down.

The fact, Mycroft remembered, letting go of Oona's hand, that we step on to the escalator . . . and we feel no jerk. But if it were still, if it had broken down and was without motion, THEN:

We would look at it.

We would tell ourselves that it was not moving.

But we would JERK.

Conditioning, Mr Pavlov, ist wünderbar!

Mycroft's hands moved crabwise down the moving rail, his long fingers, the differing speed, the treads, the rail, the fluorescent blaze above one's head and looking down one sees one's feet travelling together towards the escalator's end.

Step . . . off.

FOLLOW THE LIGHTS – blue for Waterloo
if you are a provincial
WATERLOO PADDINGTON CHARING CROSS
if you are Mycroft you know.

The Underground is very convenient, is it not? To travel hopefully – at a reasonable cost.

So down and on to the platform.

A lot of people, the backs of a great many people standing down the length of the platform – examples of raincoats, British blue, British grey, British brown.

Mycroft eyed them with the London traveller's expertise.

'A hold-up on the line.'

Oona nodded.

He was leading along the back of the crowd.

He stopped in front of the chocolate-vending machine. It was bright and red – an offering toy. Oona enjoyed her own amusement – watching the serious man deposit his sixpence in the slot.

It was returned to him.

He gave it back.

It was returned to him.

'Hit it,' Doctor Charrington suggested.

The tall narrow face calmly considers the machine. It is his only sixpence. He is a gentle and an efficient man. He deposits that sixpence for the third time and at the same instant administers a precise and accurate kick upon its metal shell. A drawer yields a mint-bright chocolate bar. Mycroft Charrington accepts it. To want is to have.

The crowd is still gathering, hemming them in. A litter basket here, and Mycroft edging towards it to deposit the wrapper. The battered evening paper (lunch-time edition) peeping from the bin. 'ULTIMATUM.' At the present time one averted one's eyes from the news.

Oona nudged him. Held out her hand. Got a piece of milk chocolate.

An afternoon of railway stations. Seeing Geoffrey off to school again just now – the special train, the boys regathering. Routine now, Oona had reminded herself, and it was routine – standing there on the self-same platform smiling at other mothers, other parents only familiar from this repeated moment. Geoffrey standing with them, a foot in each world; neither difficult in themselves now that they are both understood in their ways, but difficult for Geoffrey to maintain together.

It was a routine with an obstinate sadness.

Her own quiet reminding of the things he must remember, his ticket, his health certificate, his capacity to dream. To stand on the platform and hear his slightly over-loud greeting of other parents' sons. Her only real communication with him now, his communication with her, the tones of their voices, the expression in the eye, mother and son. Mycroft, as usual, stalking off to the head of the platform to inspect the locomotive.

The voice at last on the loudspeaker:

'Will the scholars take their seats, please.'

An afternoon of railway announcements.

'Move right down the platform, please, move right down the platform, please.' Again the certain and instructing tones of the loudspeaker.

And we move, Oona observes to herself, like sheep. But we are not sheep. Even though we stand still, with this other person's British mac not an inch from our nose, we are not sheep. Even now we experience and not only experience but ponder, and not only ponder but act upon that pondering and not only act – we enjoy – in the sense that we enjoy land – in the sense that we enjoy our function. We only slip into sheep – sometimes.

The decorations in the surgery leave something to be desired. We can light it with lamps, the pool of golden light in the middle of the room, the gleam on the instruments. And of course we arranged to have the waiting-room done first, as Mycroft suggested. Patients spend so much more time in the waiting-room.

This man in his mac is almost standing on my foot.

The fat baroness with the thick accent lying on the surgery couch with her bare bosom in the lamplight. Helga Welt suffered pain, she was alive with her interest in living, in young men's poetry, even during the waves, the gyrations of her pain, her pains that had been with her so long. Her humour was wry, she understood her heavy obese body, was fond of its peculiarities and laughed a little in the face of its inevitable change. Those sharp blue eyes taking in the quality of my own attention.

The voice on the loudspeaker that is saying the same things again.

The reflective hour after supper, talking to Mycroft over the coffee. We do not always talk about what we are doing, but also about the ideas that, like diseases, we are having. Or again we talk about nothing and we talk complete rubbish for we are in excellent health. Mycroft smiling over the coffee which he has made for us.

The smell of British blue raincoat.

They could hear no trains.

Other people against one's shoulders. People, a mass of living cells, the specialized cells of sight, the skin on the nose, the dead cells of a live girl's hair. The breathing as we all stood closer and closer together, waiting. (The girl student that once studied human people. Doctor Oona Charrington.)

No trains.

Oona's hand, Mycroft's hand, our hands, clasped.

'Do you think that the war has started?' inquired a voice, quite close to them, quite seriously.

Mycroft Charrington had a clear picture in his mind of the laboratories; the white, flat buildings, the long lines of window, the clean spaces containing communities of mice, waiting.

The conversation of backs without faces. A conversation of raincoats.

One foot was going to sleep. Waiting – a day of waiting. It had been a good holiday with Geoffrey. He had talked with his son. They had talked well. Better!

Oddly enough he found himself worried only by the fact that this journey, that this here and now should be delayed. Tomorrow, a war that might continue tomorrow, did not concern him.

Oona pushed a little leftwards in order to stay with him.

Nothing was coming.

'We can't even try to get out,' she said.

'No, there is no way out for the moment.'

They had only come down into the station the usual way, the familiar escalator as they had done so often. Upstairs it had been a Wednesday in April.

Upstairs!

The crowd was moving suddenly and for no reason, a kind of irrational no-direction. There was just time to hold Oona to be sure that she stayed with him. They were swept beyond the chocolate machine.

'My God,' someone said out loud above the scuffling silence. There was a kind of united gasp.

Oona and he were pinned up against a door. The elegant lettering of London Transport: NO ADMITTANCE.

'In here, sir,' said a voice. They were inside, in a half light of dim bulbs, and all at once the crowd was outside and on the platform and elsewhere. In the distance they could hear that loudspeaker talking again.

But their own man was saying:

'There is something of an emergency going on, sir,' and the door was closed.

They realized that he was wearing a crash helmet like a motor-cycle policeman. The goggles were down.

'Across the way here, sir, madam, quickly.' It was a compelling voice.

So there was an emergency, Mycroft thought.

Oona was only aware of a faint bewilderment, of realizing that there was no time to consider, to appreciate what was happening.

A complex set of dark-green gates folded back before them. Automatically they found themselves walking forward into the lift. The gates slid shut immediately and the helmeted figure was no longer with them. There was a slithering noise, a stomach-fluttering motion, the eerie dropping.

'We are going down,' Mycroft said quietly. He looked round at Oona. She too was examining these sudden surroundings. Like himself – it was almost too early to be surprised.

There were no advertisements in the lift. There were only plain aluminium sides and one set of gates. There were no buttons, there were no handles, there were no switches. They could not see out of the lift. But it was large, like a large room.

Only after some seconds did it occur to him that it was odd. At the far end there were two comfortable fireside chairs, with soft tapestry cushions in blues and greens and in between them a long coffee-table. An elegant coffee-pot was steaming on a tile – there were two matching cups in mottled greys, each flicked with a spray of gold. There was a plate, a mottled-grey plate with a pile of sandwiches. By the plate was a large printed envelope.

Oona stared at it and picked it up.

'It is for us,' she said, not quite believing what she saw. She handed the envelope to him. The print was not the familiar typography of London Transport.

The lift descended. There was only the sound of their movement.

'Dear darling,' Mycroft said.

Oona had sat herself in one of the tapestry chairs.

'But, Mycroft, this has all been waiting for us.'

He stood still, his long narrow face staring at hers.

'Geoffrey,' he said almost blankly. He caught a glimpse in his mind's eye of his son's dark hair – Oona's hair – the smile – the wave through the carriage window.

Here were their two selves, and the coffee and the sandwiches, descending.

Mycroft opened the envelope.

The lift was going down.

2

Berenice paused on the pavement. She was amused at herself, amused to find that she was still smiling inside. The incessant London traffic moved on beside her endlessly and within inches of where she stood by the kerb with her immense portfolio. Her fair long hair blew in her face.

The old man had liked her cartoons.

The point, the moment, the anxiety of the day had now gone, triumphantly.

She had only the irritation of steering this lumping portfolio through this unfamiliar part of London and then she could enjoy, contemplate, her recent interview.

She registered the particular tanned face of a van driver as he went leftward as she waited for the traffic lights to change.

Pick up the portfolio. Not for the first time that day, the wish to be an inch taller so that the portfolio could be carried more easily, clear of the ground. She had to bend her arm.

Stop on the island. There was a stream of traffic coming round the other way. She remembered the three nervous coffees drunk, one after the other, in the wide empty snack-bar just before the interview, hot, tasteless, unenjoyed, herself a nerve bundle. Then there had been the building, that reception area, a commissionaire, the secretary, another wait to think. She had been stupid to drink all that coffee.

'Miss Berenice Elm.'

The exhilaration of the actual interview.

Across the road again quickly. A refuse truck almost on her. Dump the portfolio on the other kerb. The brawny dustman on the back of the truck lifted a dirty gloved hand and waved it in her direction. Berenice grinned back at him. She was triumphant in her discomforts.

She began to march on along the pavement. This was, she thought, the right direction. And the old boy had asked intelligent questions, had not just reacted to a girl with a portfolio. He had seen what she had put on paper, and he had seen what she saw with her mind.

Not only the prize of accepting her work, not only giving her the job, but the better prize: comprehension.

Avoiding other people coming the other way, avoiding them with the corner of her portfolio. Couldn't they see what she was carrying? Men in bowler hats seeing a blonde girl but not seeing that she was struggling. So many people walking in the opposite direction. Onward, but an endless way to the bus stop, if she could find it.

She stopped again by the kerb. But it was heavy to carry. She was aware that she was carrying three cups of coffee.

Berenice looked at the street.

This too was Berenice!

Berenice's street with buses in their tall overbearing scarlet forging through the dusty sunshine, taxis fussing like tugs. The expression of vehicles moving, the expression of advancing headlights and radiators, chrome silver, glitter and colour, a jostle of vehicle individuals, moving downroad, signal lights winking. Tall static white cliffs of buildings reaching upward, the sides of a steep valley, the letters of an alphabet indicating business, the letters on bus blinds indicating destination, letters making words that had meaning but seen now only as letters, as shapes incised, carved, printed, painted, erected. ULTIMATUM on the newspaper proffered, shouted about, sold by the sad grey man in his overcoat in the sunshine. Sell papers from the top of an orange box. Men walking, men like marks on absorbent paper, black blobs that are bowlers – the street of Berenice.

She resisted the temptation to halt it by putting it down, by indicating the movement on paper so that it need never move from her again. Time enough. One of the side things she was learning now was to be patient, was not to eat what she saw too quickly, to let her pencil wait.

Berenice enjoyed herself walking. This was being young, the pleasure of being young and in her own street.

An inch taller . . .?

Cross another road. Dodge round the back of a taxi.

Those three coffees were pressing and the portfolio was cutting into her hand.

She, Berenice Elm, wanted to be a lady. Mother had always referred to it as 'being a lady', an effective expression for an important function with a proper touch of gentle irony.

The commissionaire at the swing doors had met her with a completely impassive face, a projection of anonymity, with a tone of respect, the embodiment of the Company.

She must admit that she enjoyed that, it did not alarm her, courtesy could be enjoyed.

And there, joy of joys, down a side-turning, a *Ladies* in the middle of the road.

Escape.

Why did they always put *Ladies* in the middle of the road? One took one's life in one's hands, and one was in a hurry.

Down the long line of very shallow scrubbed steps with the dirty green railings, the skirt tight, the portfolio bumping, the world rising above one's head, one's very own street receding. Ladies in retirement.

It was *Women* here and not ladies at all, the chipped enamel notice passing her nose. She had walked down out of the world.

The unmistakable smell, always in these places, the smell that was not quite disinfectant but a kind of amalgam of water and metal and old sluiced tiles and over used mop. Here, the glaring unilluminating light.

The female attendant, face like a headman's axe, walking down between the tall brown doors, carrying a yellow duster, landlady of all she surveyed, commentless, unseeing and disapproving. The stretch of wall with the clinical aspirin dispenser, the pale red-lettered sign giving the addresses – Albert Dock Hospital (for seamen only), the sanitary towel machine and the little poster reminding one that clean living was the only safeguard. A solitary mirror, a solitary glimpse of one's own face, fair hair awry, polo neck sweater with a slight stain.

Berenice Elm put down the portfolio, leaning it against the tall brass-furnished door. She scrabbled for a penny – coins, silver coins, threepenny bits, screwed bus tickets and a sweet paper, the coffee-bar bill and, thank God, one penny.

Drop it in, pull the bolt, push the door open (resistance of a spring), lug the portfolio inside. Slide the bolt.

ENGAGED.

One is alone, one is inside, a penny for a private world, a penny for uninvasion.

The portfolio safely propped. Tight skirts are really for men to look at, not for living, and then one sits in that half moment of expectation, of awaiting bliss.

And one's inside relaxes and there is the steady certain knowledge that one is, while one's eye moves round, over the white yellowing tiles, over the toilet paper roll, over the damp mopped concrete floor. One waits for oneself.

One is ready, one stands up feeling better, one adjusts, a sharp jerk on the chain (Bonnington's Patent No. 2) and who was Bonnington?

Back with the bolt, pull firmly at the door, hold it with one knee and pick up the dratted portfolio.

VACANT.

Emerge. Be alone no longer.

The attendant steaming forward in our direction.

'You must go out of the far door, madam, please.'

No explanation, no reason, only a blind and certain instruction.

'But I want to go out the way I came in.'

The woman did not appear to be in the least bit put out, not even surprised by this objection but neither was she deflected for a moment from her course.

'Out of the far door, madam, please.'

She was pointing and Berenice was discovering that already her own feet were obeying instructions. She was walking towards a green door at the far end.

'There is something of an emergency going on, madam.'

It was information glumly given, no alarm, no sense of actual emergency, only of orders received.

Berenice walked through the doorway, it was more modern here for the vestibule was metal lined. But there were gates at the far end and they were closed.

What did the woman mean? She put her portfolio down. She wanted to get back up to the street and this was stupid, intolerable.

But there were gates behind her, gates closing. The attendant was no longer with her. It was a lift, a slithering noise of vertical movement.

Perhaps this was the best way out.

It was only after some seconds that it occurred to her that anything was odd.

The lift was going down.

3

Brother Nicholas walked where he had been instructed. He was a small, lithe man and now, just occasionally, he could see his own reflection as he passed the South Kensington shop windows. He observed himself in his brown habit, the heavy wooden rosary at his belt and the sandals. He observed, not only himself he reflected, but also his own comical curiosity about himself. But one proceeded, kindly yet without comment, unanswering and in charge of one's own particular and curious self.

Here the vehicles, the unfamiliar traffic, were majestic and in flaring colour, the road wide, the mid-afternoon movement comparatively light. He considered it while he crossed the road and on the ample pavement he was not concerned.

Now there were no shop windows and his feet proceeding – a breeze touching his tonsured head. He had been instructed.

Research, in which he was engaged, was not an important word in the Community. It was a function, sometimes required, a means to a patient and unhurried end, an end that is not necessarily to be reached in this generation.

Here was the Victoria and Albert Museum. He turned right and under the rounded archway. The sandals walked up the steps. To enter was almost an ecclesiastical sensation, the hushed vastness, the high building, the sound of other people's footfalls.

Brother Nicholas had a particular purpose, and he could remember the general direction in which the gallery lay. Through here – under an archway, and one was being encircled by a great round chamber. Here were the warm greens of a sumptuous chasuble – an unfamiliar curve of a bishop's crozier – wrought and old and splendidly illuminated . . . things and objects suspended behind glass.

Brother Nicholas hardly paused. He registered. It was true to say, he supposed, that he understood these things. In his House he was the keeper of many marvellous things. He had been told, and he remembered, that even the beautiful was not always important. He walked onward through this gallery –

– he was uncertain

– he turned right.

Along another gallery and then he knew he was in the wrong place for this was the Far Eastern Room. Yet this too he understood, here too he was brought up sharply, for he was recalled to his interest in these things before he joined his Order.

Here, he judged, magnificence was not the word, rather there was a commanding and balanced calm, a collection of muted objects and of poised deliberation. None of the things that were here drew attention to themselves. Bowls and jade hung timeless at one's gaze. A Bodhissatva in palest stone with the faintest flush of reds upon its surface sat and was seated in compassion and observation, always compassion and always observation before the Brother in his habit, and Nicholas knew the reasons for this object here.

He permitted himself the single indulgence of walking round, of seeing the great thrones, the rabbits painted on silk, the altar furniture, and then he left the gallery and tried again.

Research was a not unimportant duty.

He found his way, Christ on a donkey, angels made in wood, glass in such colours that he did not read their story, their depiction, he saw only this window.

Here was a gallery that opened out on to the museum quadrangle. Here within was a figure of the Virgin. The museum had only lately acquired her, had only lately put her on display. She had been discovered, with great excitement, the previous year on the excavation of the crypt of a tiny church.

She was a disturbing figure. Brother Nicholas had expected that he would be disturbed. Perhaps this was why she had been so buried. It was not that this Mary was unbeautiful but that she might be dangerous to see. She stood in her blue (a battered worn and ancient blue) looking bold, looking curiously provocative, a girl's body definite under her garment – Mary in her kilt they called her – her arms akimbo, her feet slightly apart, carved hands, carved feet. This was indeed a girl and yet this was Mary – this was the irresistible power of uttermost mercy – this Mary could out-countenance the world.

But what did I expect, Nicholas asked himself, and for the moment looked away, half looked away, looked really at himself.

He walked round to the other side. He looked again, quietly and without hurry. He would say, in his description, that if it was not certain that she was Mary, it was still certain that she was a work of art. Certainly she was not the usual view, but could she not yet be different and yet a true vision of Our Lady?

Brother Nicholas sat down. It was a convenient seat. The museum seemed to be particularly empty.

Outside the sun was shining into the quadrangle. It was good to sit and look.

She was about ten and a half inches high. Some peasant girl, no doubt, had been used for the model.

She stood there, hands on her hips, an unreleased spring, a latent final energy, a half smile of expecting happiness, a looking of powerful waiting confidence that could destroy the distance into which it stared. It was as if something was about to happen of inexplicable horror with which she would be able, and she alone, to have business, to endure, to utterly surmount.

He took out his black covered notebook.

Then again, Nicholas considered, suppose that one went away from the first impact from this first figure. Supposing that one considered the life of Our Lady, both as to what had been and what was yet to come. Could not one say that in the final analysis this Mary spoke in a way that was most true, that this spoke of the eternal Mary rather than the Mary of those years in an outlying district of the Roman empire, that she spoke not of the Mary that was only the mother but also of the Mary that was woman. Not the woman of too many men's ideals. (Too many women modelled themselves on too many men's ideals.) But woman as she actually was.

Who am I, Brother Nicholas wondered, to pontificate on this?

An attendant was coming towards him.

But perhaps it was not an attendant. It appeared to be a motor-cycle policeman in a crash helmet. When he was a boy he had wanted to be a motor-cycle policeman. Wrrrrrrm! Wrrrrrrm!

'I have been following you, sir, for the last five-eighths of a mile through a built-up area . . .'

The man was in fact walking straight towards him.

'This way, sir. This way I am afraid. You can't stay here.'

Brother Nicholas had been trained for fifteen years that one did not speak unless it was necessary. For the present it did not seem necessary to question. This was the voice of authority. Had something occurred? Perhaps it was idle to inquire. Wordless he closed his notebook and followed. He left the Mary.

'There's a bit of an emergency in process,' the crash helmet said. 'Through this way, sir. It will be safer down here.'

He unlocked a faceless door. There were stone steps tightly winding down.

Nicholas descended. The helmeted figure did not follow him. He had reclosed the door. They seemed appropriate steps. The sound of one's sandals made a familiar monastic sound. The spiral was dimly lit. It went down.

It went down a long way.

There was an occasional light.

'It must lead to a shelter,' Nicholas patiently decided.

It went down.

The stairs curled unexpectedly to an end. There was a sense of stone cellar. He could only walk forward. In front of him there was an open doorway that led through to a single cell seven feet long by seven feet wide. It was painted white. There was a single plain crucifix on the wall. On the floor there was a pitcher of water and a brown loaf of bread beside a small wooden stool. There was nothing else, he thought.

Nicholas entered.

Quietly and behind him a gate closed. There was a slithering noise, a stomach-fluttering motion, an eerie dropping.

He was in a lift.

There was something else. By the pitcher of water there was a large printed envelope.

The lift was going down.

4

It had been a long time.

Fingers trailed down within him and tightened

The drop.

He remained on his knees.

'O Lord have mercy upon us.'

Nicholas no longer knew what time was. He knew only the plain white walls, the wooden stool, the empty pitcher and the crumbs upon the floor.

Eating was comforting.

At last there was a distinct and gripping check to the descent, a long pneumatic sigh, a gasp, and the cell was motionless. The gates were behind him when they opened. Nicholas stood up. He did not know whether to believe or whether not to believe the grey printed letter. A warm air was blowing into the interior of the lift and on to his neck. He turned round, but slowly.

The Order to which his Community belonged had always been both patient and unhurried.

Beyond the gates he could see what was at first only a gentle swaying of softly golden light, a light diffused with blotches and shadows. He became richly aware of the strong scents of vegetation.

He walked out of the lift.

The gate closed behind him. Instantly.

He jumped a little – in spite of himself. So he must walk on. Almost he did not notice it but he had walked out into a world.

He stood looking through under trees. During the descent he had read that there would be a certain beauty here.

Everywhere there were these trees, but trees whose great trunks were palely translucent green, whose leaves, narrow and endless, were a polished bronze and hung high above his head in the soft light coming down, coming through. The warm air, and it was warm, moved over him. He could feel both the sense of distance and of complete enclosure. He was looking down under a roof. This light, he decided, must be dazzling above, but here it was a filtered gold. Straight before him between the soaring trunks holding up their tent of leaves the ground was leading steeply down. Here was a path made with steps at intervals, and Nicholas found himself following it.

'I will go in this direction.'

Again he knew his nose. Now it seemed a sharp flavour on the air, more a taste than a smell, and he found himself with an intoxication that filled him with a bubbling rush of well-being, that gave him the sudden desire to move, to shout, to run.

He skipped.

This pulled him up sharply.

Brother Nicholas walked firmly down the path, feeling himself to be smiling, but he was careful, he was a little bewildered. Yet this place was joyous, happily alarming, the ground was sprung under the feet.

He was being invited. He must apply – discretion. He was alone, so pleasantly alone, he was imbued with being free, there was no duty, no order, no time for each succeeding action, no fear of limitless time.

The steps ceased for the floor had flattened, and now ahead the path appeared to be closed by a deliberate curtain of massed blossoms, blossoms with deep velvet petals and crimson vertical creeper that was – splashed, interlaced when he was nearer, with rainbow-coloured leaves or again half-silvers and steel blues that edged around the purples and deep brown. Soft colour everywhere here imposed and smothered over dominant bronze. He enjoyed pressing colour apart, aside, in order to proceed down his path.

He was becoming aware of what he had been hearing since he had arrived, of what he was hearing – a distant playing of complex bells that rang and rose and came up and fell solemnly away, almost to disappear, to begin again, as if now from a different direction, a saddened noble tolling that regretted, that knew sorrow, that would rise up and then pause – to tinkle away into distant silver and retreat again.

In the distance he thought he saw a form moving, but it was not true, there were flowers, he could see nothing running. Persistently he was happy. His feet – his feet cried out to go leaping.

He walked carefully.

The path curved a little through this tunnel of blossom to skirt one of the great tree trunks. The translucent bark was a milk-like green, shot just here and there with the occasional vein of gold. It was warm to the touch. He had put out his hand. He had stopped. He was putting his lips against it, against the green surface of the trunk. How it was there! But as trees these things were impossible.

These trees had not been planted at regular intervals. He was certain that they had been placed. They were made. It was as if they were carved in jade. Delicately, gently, even on this huge scale, they were constructed.

Yet the blossoms seemed real enough. The creepers were growing, he picked up a leaf and surely it was alive. There was sap. He dropped the leaf and walked forward. It was like walking through curtains of flowers, he was parting and parting them with his hands. Was the path leading him into a maze? Their fragrance was heavy in his head.

Brother Nicholas looked firmly in front of him.

Yet when he came to look at himself he was happy. A carillon was still sounding, delicate, half-heard, a long way from the ear. He did not ask where the path led, this colour, these streamers of flowers, of dangling silvered petals and lines of scent. They touched his mouth and his face as he plunged forward. They trailed over his habit, he was not concerned as to where he was going.

And then he was through. He had emerged from the curtain. All at once he was in a new clearing.

It was immense, a great space softly carpeted with a deep smooth covering of copper-like grass, a sward that led gently down like the sides of a huge shallow saucer, a saucer holding one end of a lake at its centre – a wide pool of still surface that surrounded an apparently motionless column of falling water, dropping from the high roof and sliding downward in complete silence.

Nicholas realized that this was not a true clearing. It was only that these pillars, columns, trees, stood more apart, rose higher, that the arches, domes and branches curved more steeply.

Far away – down by the edge of the gilded water – he could see a girl. He was drunk with air.

And this incredible column of water shimmering and falling and the distant figure of this girl crouched and gazing downward into it.

Nicholas halted – half moved to go forwards, to go backward.

She was waiting for him.

She was crouching by the water edge, looking intently, not at the scene but with a fascinated waiting interest at the molten reflection of herself. He saw that she was dressed in black, a sweater, a skirt, the legs bare, the feet naked, her shoes abandoned in the grass. She crouched there, not seeing him, but just gazing.

It seemed simple and self-evident that he must go up to her and speak.

The distant bell changing, no he could discover no melody, he strained to listen, it was dying away. It was behind him. But now in front, beyond the lake somewhere, behind the scenes, there was a new crescendo coming . . .

She had fair hair falling over one shoulder, a mass of long corn-coloured hair and it was a long time since he had deliberately spoken to a girl.

As he walked forward the warmth was pleasant and around him. He noticed a large portfolio lying on its side in the grass near her. It was evident that she was waiting. His sandals moved sternly over the gleaming unfamiliar lawn, taking him towards her.

Standing where she was, even crouching down and listening intently, Berenice still found that she could not hear the fall of the water, the polished slide of tons of descending liquid. But she could hear someone coming. The extraordinary, the almost fascinating, the by now almost taken for granted loneliness and spell of this place was about to have a new dimension. At last – but there was a return, like a shadow, of her first fear.

But even now she was carried by this spell, carried away by the sight of golden water falling, by the stately motionless leaves floating on the pool's surface.

Yet she had heard someone.

She had been sorry to leave her lift. That had become, instead of a prison, a known and familiar place. Then she had walked to this lake, she had kicked off her shoes and had got rid of her stockings like a little girl and had pulled up her skirt and had dabbled her feet. This too had become hers. She had looked back and had seen only the blue smooth cliffs going up to the bronze roof.

She could hardly remember the traffic and the street.

Now she had heard someone.

Berenice forced herself to turn round. For an instant it was like living in one of those second-rate horror films that Bruce was always delighting in taking her to in the Tottenham Court Road.

'Ahhhhhhh!'

The face was of a mild, a cautious but steadily determined man, a man smaller than herself, but a monk –

– with one of those heads –

– coming towards her with an Establishment expression.

She could hear only the sound of her own voice, such a little voice, very little for Berenice's voice, a tiny blurt:

'They have sent you to tell me, haven't they – I suppose I'm dead – aren't I?'

The noise of the chorus had completely died away. There was complete silence.

This idea of death had obviously never entered the little man's head. Never.

But might it not be possible . . .?

She could see, actually see his mind considering her suggestion. A new thought.

And then he was saying that he did not think so, that he did not think she was dead. He wasn't laughing at her.

Perhaps it was absurd to be dead and to enjoy having one's feet out of one's best shoes.

Actually he had a nice face.

Actually she had a nice face even if for a moment it

had been frightened. He looked quietly out at this girl's face and knew, even now, that she had been sent to wait for him. A temptation? Not, he thought, so simple as a temptation. He must remember that in charity he must make no judgement. For him he had only to observe.

Brother Nicholas rubbed his nose. Perhaps, he reflected, the nose itches even after death. Perhaps, even in death, one can savour the acute sensual pleasure of the good scratch. Also, he noted, he was still enjoying his own continuing calm. All things sweep by and yet still he knew the reality of what and who he was.

His previous continuing and ordered life did not cease for his absence; the smiling lowered head of Brother John now grey, and the sound of footsteps down well-polished corridor, the Prior tall and standing abstracted in a doorway (so often abstracted, so often failing, so much beloved), the continued hoeing of weeds in the monastic garden.

'Christ have mercy upon us.

Kyrie eleison.

Christie eleison.

Christie eleison.'

'But,' the girl was saying, 'you have been sent to me. They said in their letter that somebody would come. I just don't know where I am.'

'Nor I,' Nicholas heard himself say. 'I am as amazed as you are. They left me a letter and so you see I am expecting – someone. Perhaps I am expecting you.'

They just stood looking at each other. They were remembering again what was about them – the tall carved trunks that lifted up into the . . . leaves above them. They were a monk and a girl standing by the edge of a long lake into which a column of shimmering water streamed without a sound. The girl's feet, and his own feet still dusty from Kensington, stood on this grass. They were two persons in an impossible landscape.

'My name's Berenice,' she was saying, almost like himself uncertain and intoxicated with new experience. She sat in the grass in front of him. She sat carelessly, skirt high and her knees apart like a boy, perhaps because she was a little tired, a little drunk. He looked away from her legs. She was attractive in spite of being drunk, of being overwhelmed by the extraordinary – even he was extraordinary, he remembered – shocked by the awful situation. (Awe – that effective, that out-of-date word.) He allowed himself to look up at the features of the girl, the turned-up nose, the keen pale brownness of the skin.

'I am called Nicholas,' he admitted.

'And what are we to do – Nicholas?' she said and it was at once an experiment, a careful listening to the sound of his name pronounced by her own voice, rather than a question.

She was seizing his hand in her girl's hand and was grasping it. He could feel her individual fingers.

'What are we to do?' she again asked him to tell her, but it still wasn't a real question.

There had been parties that, unexpectedly, she had particularly enjoyed. Enjoyment came from the un-expected, unsought reason, the things that had not been looked for, had been granted, like a grace. There had been that quaint pyjama party in Gwen's walled garden on that glorious June evening, with the scent of roses, huge pale yellow roses, people in paisley patterns, crimsons and blues worn by staid familiars, the girls in demure pink with buttons sweetly left undone. There had been no hurry either to drink or to talk but an ocean of time in which to do both or neither. It had been warm, very warm. It had been difficult to feel particularly wicked with that lazy evening sunshine in a garden full of Gwen's polite sculpture. One just sat and watched golden red-haired Kathy, naked to the waist, shyly serving pots of Gwen's punch from a plain wooden tray. Some of the guests had been drawing her. The music had sounded in the very far distance. A young and noble lord had photographed a rose. (Dear Stephen, in scarlet silk.) While Bruce, in his conservative broad blue striped, with a cord, Kathy's milky bosom not a foot away, his voice as always talked in tones rather than with a meaning. They had drunk the punch from Kathy's peculiar pots. Berenice had watched the foxgloves lit in the glow of the open french window, the dusk falling, time and an asparagus sandwich, the enjoyment of flavour on the tongue, within the mouth – grass on the feet.

Grass on the feet.

'Are you hungry,' he was asking her, his hands emerging from the sleeves of his habit. 'That is the first thing.' He was quiet-eyed, unhurried, but prepared to establish a direction.

'I know where there is some fruit,' Berenice volunteered.

She got up again. He found she was taking him by the hand. Her energy was returning to her again. She led him along the edge of the lake. For an instant he paused to look more intently at the smooth quivering column of falling water. It was impossible to tell where it came from. She pulled a little at his hand to make him follow. It was like towing a small dog.

'But you have left your portfolio behind,' he pointed out. He had noticed, he had remembered her property.

'It's not far,' she explained. She was absurdly cheerful again. This place made one almost frighteningly cheerful. He is nice, Berenice thought. She had never really thought about monks before. Oddly enough Kathy had been a Catholic, so had Gwen. 'Religion's just a substitute for art,' Bruce had told her. She towed her monk away from the lake now, back towards another flowering garden at the foot of a pillar. Blossoms and small trees clustered all round its base.

'I found them when I first arrived,' she explained. She had felt quite mad when she had first arrived. She was Berenice again now. In spite of. She enjoyed being Berenice.

They were apricots.

She could reach much higher than he could.

She could reach much higher than he could.
Eating is comforting.

She had stopped laughing. She was not looking at the apricots.

She had forgotten herself, portfolio, everything.

Berenice was looking across the apricot branches. She looked slowly, almost perhaps without comprehension.

'I did not see that the first time,' she said.

'See what?'

She pointed.

He could not see from where he stood so that he had to stand beside her. She was looking between the branches.

From here he now saw that the pool narrowed and swept away almost like a river. At the far end, and it was a long way away, it opened out again. Along the shining neck of the water the pillars flanked its edges so that it had all the appearance of a great nave, but at the far end where it widened the trunks rose like stilts out of the water itself. On the further bank, and also seeming to be growing out of the water, stood a house. It was large. Even at this distance one could see – it was of this place. Perhaps, impossibly, it was blown glass. It was multi-coloured, curved and domed and delicately swelling and yet not round but long with veins of colour, with windows merging into walls, transparent, opalescent, opaque, blues and greys and veined with red.

'A place,' Berenice breathed. 'Somewhere. We must go to it.' She grabbed his hand again. 'Come on.'

'Your portfolio first,' Nicholas said quietly.

'Sod the portfolio – there is nobody to take anything

here. I want to be free. Oh! I am sorry.' She let go of his hand.

'Why are you sorry?'

'I did not mean to use that word.'

'But it was in your mind – it expressed a meaning to you. It is the meaning in your mind that is important. I'll carry your portfolio for you.'

He strode away to be back in a few moments but he had to admit that it was heavier than he expected. The girl was smiling at his insistence, he was shorter than she was – it would be more difficult for him to carry, and then they left the apricot garden, skirting a wide tree trunk and all at once the house came into view.

Berenice found that he was leading.

'Do you think that we are – do you think that we are meant to go there?' she said to him.

'They forbid me nothing in my letter except that I must not attempt to leave, unless requested. We are not trying to leave. We do not know where we are. What does it matter where we go?'

They were walking on metallic grass again. Perhaps shyly, out of some sense of loneliness, he found her coming alongside him, searching for his free hand, and he let her take it.

'And who are THEY?' he asked her, asked himself, but she did not answer, she just walked unencumbered beside him. They walked under these high trees, the green jade pillars, under the solemn gold, and there was nobody in sight.

'There are birds here,' Nicholas exclaimed.

A duck was paddling on the still water, a busy tug-like motion, going in a particular direction. Nicholas was only aware of happiness again, of something wonderful, an intangibility bubbling in his mind. Caution had become a difficulty.

The slow water-mill of the monastery rumbling and Brother John moving bags with an easy confident strength – Nicholas always required more effort than John – and the water flowing far beneath their feet and the lush banks beyond and the mill's tall timbers and St Basil carved and battered high above the roof beams, the turn of the heavy mechanism . . .

'I am liking that house,' Berenice was announcing. Her rope of fair hair swung across her shoulders as her head moved. She was a girl and interested.

'Do you see the way the house rests on its site? As if it had been placed! And I've only seen glass used like that before with tiny objects. Those greys and blues, like Roman glass.' (Nicholas was nodding. He knew.) 'It comes outward from its inside, those domes come outwards. There are no struts, no supports, only itself, like a bowl. It gives the sense of having grown. There is also the other way round – it goes down into itself. There is an aliveness. I want to feel it inside.'

There was nobody in sight, no sign of occupation, no smoke, no light, only the level golden light from the 'ceiling'.

41

'Those are not barn doors, they are clear windows,' Berenice was saying.

Brother Nicholas walked silently beside her, methodically calming his own absurd joy. He had not noticed barn doors.

The house was built high like a stranded ship with a deck from which a delicate metallic stairway led down to the still surface of the lake. The symmetrical position of the house within four of the rising pillars served to emphasize its own curious artificiality. Yet there were yellow blossoms clambering about the glass walls, imprecise and growing.

They walked on together and now they were near enough their side of the lake to be able to make out the details of the house, the long high clear windows under the grey veined turbid glass of its curving upperworks, the glass sides that were coloured, stained at different levels and depths within its thickness, a bubble like a battleship.

'What do we want a house to do?' Nicholas asked out loud, asking really of himself. It was a question to which Berenice obviously had an answer and one that he must now ask himself. Yet was he in fact a novice, was he in fact out of any sort of depth?

'I am going to find out what this house does,' she replied.

'Do you think we should be cautious?' He seemed more interested in her attitude than in an actual need for caution.

'No. I think we just have to go there.'

42

For the present it was possible that she was correct. He had almost overlooked that they were in someone's, something's power all the time.

He had patience.

She increased her stride.

She had a long stride for a girl, he thought. The portfolio was heavy.

He had only been down here for a little while, in this glorious warm light. He attended to the scents invading his nose. Now the bells could be reheard, a very long way away, very softly, but a different ringing, an invitation, an inviting. He wondered about it.

'I can see no movement inside,' Berenice was telling him.

They had reached the edge of the lake at the point nearest to the house. There were lilies here, paling flesh white and floating with flat black leaves. The other shore, with the silver spider stairs, was perhaps only a hundred yards away from them.

'Look,' Berenice pointed. Away to the right the lake swung like a great bow round the back of the house as it swung to the left around the front. Berenice left him and ran along the lake edge. Brother Nicholas watched her, enchanted with her running. She reached a point where she could see across and then stopped dead.

'It's on an island,' she called. He heard her above the sound of the chorus. It was odd to hear this now familiar voice calling back to him. He stood where he was and she walked back.

'It's on a complete island,' her voice repeated.

43

'Do you think we should call?' Nicholas suggested.

She nodded.

After a moment they both hallooed. Perhaps it was their imagination but the sound of the bells seemed to get louder at the same moment. They hallooed again, her voice, his own. There was no reply.

Nicholas realized that there was a punt moored to a floating landing stage at the bottom of those stairs.

'That boat is on the other side. Logically you would think then that somebody is at home.' He went on looking at the house. Somehow he did not believe that anyone was there.

Berenice was on the very edge of the lake, looking down between the lilies and then up towards the house.

'It's so near,' she said. 'Do you think I could swim over and bring that boat across?'

'There is nowhere else for us to go,' Nicholas agreed out aloud.

She moved, he noticed, from a dependence on him to a desire to look after him. There was in her a half-hidden assumption that he was helpless. And he was glad to have put her portfolio down. He stopped thinking just for a moment and sat restfully in the curious grass. His mind stopped raising problems. He saw a dragon-fly hovering, an intense blue thing, not a foot from his nose and wonderful. So there were insects down here. A complete if artificial ecology. . . . He was pondering again. He stretched his feet in his sandals. What was the time? he wondered. He had not brought any of the apricots. He wished he had.

44

The brown face puckered round the nose.

'O.K.?' it was asking him.

'O.K.,' the monk said gravely.

He would not embarrass her by deliberately looking away. She peeled off down to the girl animal quite quickly and methodically. (He realized that of course she had never picked her shoes up when they had gone to look for the fruit – he would not volunteer to go back for her at this stage.) Underneath her clothes she was fairly brown, she had not shaved the fair hair under her arms. She stood there, gauging the distance, overlooking the water, absently fingering the twisted fur on her tummy.

'Here goes,' she said quite simply, and plumped in, feet first, in among the lilies.

Nicholas both watched and remembered, without regret, remembering his own girl cousins, Margaret and Astrid, laughing at him kindly when he had first seen them. They had been older than he had been, they were all changing together in the garden between the cliffs, red-headed girls, really just the same when he got used to them without their things on, and always talking. He was remembering too the other garden (he did not dig it, he was not a gardener) with its continued quiet contemplation, the Brothers there compassionate, steady, undisturbed by each other, the knowledge of what was past, what was present; here the quiet in-waiting of all time that is the Monastery. Here, the Prior had reminded him years ago, there is not only religion, here is yourself. Respect it. Or his girl cousins naked and talking fiercely about ponies. They had respected him. Nicholas was a good rider.

Berenice swam neatly, striking out beyond the lilies. There was no sound again, he realized, only the splash of her swimming.

'It's warm,' she called. 'Absurdly warm.' She was wading the last few yards, emerging from the water, the fair hair soaking. She did not find it difficult to climb into the punt.

No one appeared. The house looked down, empty, large-windowed, transparent and curved and still – but very real, and waiting, incredibly waiting.

Berenice had found a paddle. She pushed the squat and heavy punt out into the stream. It began to nose towards him.

Turn the nose towards him. He sits there waiting, so peacefully, so unaffected, so particularly contained, her little monk. One could contain him in nine, five strokes of an inky brush, portray him like a Chinese sage sitting. Sensible, undeniably sensible, she admitted. Sensible, Berenice pondered, and not just common-sensical but understanding. 'Sensible' was one of those words that one could think about, that crept out on one side of one's mind and whispered 'sensibility', a special capacity to receive.

The punt slid noiselessly over the still water and she could see only gold, the smooth pillars of the nearest trees lofting upward, bending high in distant curves and archways. And almost for the first time she was being looked at without either that outraged rejection or greediness as if she was an approaching feast. She was being accepted, appreciated even, but allowed to be herself. Brother Nicholas was peculiarly civilized. He was up and grasping at the sloping prow as she crunched in over the lilies. His feet were wet. They lifted the portfolio into the punt between them. (This morning she had had an interview.) He handed her her clothes. He lifted them with his fingers with an unaccustomed care. She dropped them into the bottom of the boat. She was still wet, but wonderfully, joyfully warm.

'Come on, I'll push off,' she said to him. It was an adventure together. The bells were dying, were rising, were chiming, were fading away again.

She sloshed back into the luscious gold water and shoved and then joined him, water running off her, coming into the punt on one brown knee. He had found the pole.

'I can do this,' Nicholas said to her, smiling. She slid herself down at his feet as he swung the punt round with an almost contemptuous ease.

The prow turned towards the high translucent house, the pillars reaching upward above the great lawns, a sense of endless green June colleges and a girl sprawled in one's boat, a private cargo for an afternoon. Droplets of water still clung to her breasts and she was obviously happy and he was drunk. He thrust hard at the lake bottom.

There was a loud black fluttering over their heads and the grating calls of dark birds flying high and frantically rising. Nicholas looked up as they went over them and then back to where they had come from.

They were in midstream but he stopped poling.

'Look,' he said quietly. They both watched. A tall man and a woman holding his hand were walking towards the edge of the lake, to the point that they had just left.

They looked, they were dressed, they were quite ordinary. The man was carrying an overcoat. But they came forward with a quiet confidence.

Berenice looked at them intently, but like Nicholas himself, she was not alarmed.

'Perhaps these are the people,' she suggested, 'the people we are supposed to see.'

Once more Brother Nicholas swung the punt round. As he turned it the panorama of the house swung too before his eyes. He could not hear, he did not think he could hear, the carillon's sound, it seemed to be silent now, but he could clearly, very clearly, remember their invitation. To turn seemed almost impossible but they must speak to these people. He could hear the dark birds still complaining and wheeling and now far away.

The tall man was waving.

Behind them was the endless space, the gold and the patches of blossom.

Berenice sat still, still naked, watching them, interested.

'They like each other,' she said.

Nicholas thrust at the pole.

5

He watched the punt move in towards the bank. The
monk watched him in return with an acute, a steady
balancing curiosity.

So far, Mycroft reflected, the adventure had proceeded
according to some meticulous and ordered plan, but it
was not his plan. He observed both his own cautious
pleasure in that the girl was at once naked and charming,
factors not always found to coincide; and in the intellec-
tual contemplation of the striking and presumably
intended compliment she made to the presence of a
grave and tonsured monk. Already – he ticked the factors
on the fingers of his mind – the exact meeting at the exact
moment at Piccadilly: the comfortable waiting lift, the
printed and explicit letter that conveyed so little.

'We move onward,' Oona was murmuring so that only
he could hear, 'towards our next impossibility.' She had a
saying not infrequently quoted before her daily consulta-
tions: 'The unusual we rely upon to happen every day;
the impossible, by contrast, only happens seven times a
week.'

.   .   .

Their impossible arrival: sitting at ease, hiding their anxieties from each other, the back lash pull at the stomach of a suddenly slowing lift. In a lift there are no windows, nothing to tell one about one's speed, one's whereabouts, only the sense of descent. No idea as to what one would see . . .

The gates opening. They stand together.

The first thing they had seen, that they had stared at almost stupidly: a huge clump of waxen scarlet elongated flowers.

They had felt the first warmth on their faces, they had walked, had almost tottered out of their lift – the golden shadowy world all about them. Then the gates had closed behind but they had been looking up, up at the polished blue-grey cliff rising high and sheer. They had been too overwhelmed . . . 'splendour' – the word had come like a light into his mind.

'Look, Mycroft. Look.' Oona squatting in the golden grass, a girl again, playing with a little white woolly creature, the size of a lap-dog with a long neck.

'This place doesn't exist. This creature isn't. Look, Mycroft. It's herbivorous. See the little hooves.'

And it galloped and galloped and gambolled and then started away, crashing in miniature through ultramarine ferns, a tiny lama, one foot high.

'How Geoffrey would love it,' she had exclaimed and she paused.

They had forgotten to be worried. The lama re-appeared, running downhill. They followed it though it was too warm to give chase. In the very far distance

Mycroft could catch the glint of water. It was intoxicating it was wonderful to walk together.

If only he could ask someone a question.

Now was his opportunity.

'Good afternoon,' Mycroft began. It was an excellent English custom. In one moment he would be hearing the sounds of their voices, he would hear them speaking.

'Hello,' said the naked girl in the boat. It was a slightly bubbling, an amused voice.

And: 'Good afternoon,' the monk was replying. It was, Mycroft noted, that very particular, very Catholic upper-class accent that is so equally confident, yet so distinctly of a slightly different place.

He had heard them speak. But the girl was starting again.

'The question is, have you been waiting for us or are we all just meeting up by accident? You see I was in the City only this morning.'

The punt lay almost motionless out on the water.

'I was at South Kensington – in a museum,' the monk stated.

There was a very distinct pause. Mycroft could hear a bird trilling high and intensely in the background. He could also hear Oona saying: 'Well we were in the tube station at Piccadilly.' They were all beginning to laugh. Mycroft was laughing himself. He was standing there clutching an overcoat with tropical blossoms hanging down all round him.

'Don't you get the feeling,' he suggested gently, 'that – that we just seem to keep on hitting new questions without finding any answers?' He spoke to himself really. Oona was used to it.

'It is very real,' the monk said. 'It continues to be frighteningly real.'

'Do you know where you are going?' the girl asked.

'We just saw the house,' Oona replied. 'We thought we might find somebody. We were told, in our letter, that we would meet someone.'

Mycroft just stood still, gazing up towards the shimmering bubble-like house, taking it in, ignoring them now, looking.

'We have not been in it yet,' the monk offered. 'We have shouted across, but there was no response and Berenice had to swim over to get the punt. We were just about to explore when you appeared.' He smiled. 'They call me Brother Nicholas,' he added as an afterthought.

Berenice dropped casually back into the water and began to push the punt close in.

Mycroft suddenly came to.

'The word extraordinary is a little overworked today,' he said almost apologetically. 'Here can I give you a hand with that?'

'We're Charrington,' Oona was saying. 'This is my husband Mycroft. I'm Oona.'

She watched her husband helping to beach the punt. He had dropped the overcoat, he was in his patched old sports jacket, food stained, work stained, apparently hanging on his back. He seemed, as usual, to grasp at the boat so awkwardly and yet it came smoothly ashore when he pulled. As usual she saw his glance move slowly, over Brother Nicholas and then over this girl, crowsfeet forming at the corner of each eye.

Mycroft tasted both men and women like a senior Frenchman tasting wine. He conceived them – he admitted to seeing them – as a kind of emotional diagram, as a series of lines expressing an exact combination of need, tension, pleasure, balance, satisfaction – which led to understanding – a whole hierarchy of understandings. They made for him a psycho-social-emotive continuum, a cross-word structure for his lust to understand.

Unexpectedly holidays would suddenly be demanded in the middle of the long bouts of fog-bound bone waiting research. Oona would find herself standing with him, her hand in his, while they watched a brown old man packing a pipe. The man sat bent and arched on the stone wall along the quay, a subjective centre for the pleasure of this nicotine, this experience of a long life, that enjoyment later of plain food. They watched, while Mycroft spoke to him, the sharp-faced local brats climbing and sliding in and out of the water, owning the harbour, female children yelling orders. (Exuberance, the expenditure of energy, the enjoyment without reflection, the enjoyment almost without knowing.) Dear Mycroft, the slow glances, the slow questions, the measuring, the noting what was about him. Their own son, Geoffrey, the boy's eyes grey-green, distance staring, drying vaguely, naked behind a rainbow towel. (Mycroft watching the boy – crowsfeet sharpening in his look.) The boy looking inward and outward, he has a mind of his own. You must have a mind of your own, a world for the Gods to dwell in. Oona remembered drying Geoffrey, the boy's body firm under her hand. Her mind was unspoken at this instant, now that he was not here – at that instant in the past while father and son talked about boats, their eyes watching girls diving. It was sufficient that Geoffrey, that Mycroft, existed. Mycroft smiling, his hand on Geoffrey's shoulder, watching each movement, the old man smoking, the jumping children, turning it all into a pattern, a network of symbols in his mind.

Mycroft, now silent beside Oona, adding each new observation to his total record.

And there was his other collection, the row of connecting laboratories that were white and clean and glassed-in and subdivided and sterile – containing mice. Here there were endless mice with differing colours, breeding, eating, scuttling, dying of carefully modified diseases (rather like men) or not dying: those that did not die – they raised the question. Quiet and sensible women in white smocks numbered and noted them, examined each mouse and recorded it each day. Each mouse had a number, a description. Oona had visited this place, Mycroft's place, had stepped over the endless mouse-proof walls, had watched a little brindled creature running round her husband's careful hand.

'Each one is a small potential tragedy,' Mycroft had said, 'a small individual giving us one tiny link to the chain that may draw up our answer – and there is the occasion when even the wrong answer can produce a fascinating insight.'

Perhaps it was only through Mycroft that Oona had learnt so consciously to enjoy, to observe, to taste sheer health for its own sake. They would stand watching a young brown woman, her step, the carriage of her head, the pad of her sandals down the marine arcade, the swing of her full blue denim skirt. They would enjoy Geoffrey asleep on the sand.

'A human being is a flavour.'

'The final object of scientific research is not so much to inform or educate or even understand – rather it is to . . . intrigue other minds.'

(At another level I can intrigue – only myself. Of anything else, of anyone else: there is no certainty.)

Oona had thought of Mycroft, and had described for him her own careful examination, in her surgery, in their own house, of an eleven-year-old girl, legs pitifully paralysed, the wisp-like white helpless face, trusting yet shrinking a little from the confident Doctor Charrington touch. The creature lay on the couch, a function but so unable, uncovered, and already beginning to turn from a helpless girl into a hopeless woman. Oona had described how she had seen, in the middle of the examination, little Matilda begin to vomit, how the girl's frame had not really the strength to be sick with gusto, how the face only increased its usual sad distress and the girl's stomach emptied itself out of the side of her mouth. Carefully the head had been held, young hair, soft indecisive coloured hair and the mouth had dribbled sickness and patiently the mouth, the couch, the flesh, had been cleaned.

Matilda had stayed awhile, recovering a little. Mycroft had talked to her, his grey eyes amused, his stories of the habits of hedgehogs and elephants. She liked him.

Brother Nicholas watched him help his wife into the punt. He picked up his coat and Nicholas took it from him and put it on the portfolio. Mycroft swung a laborious leg aboard.

New ducks were coming round the lake edge to join in the floating, fancy ducks these, painted like galleons, making short remarks one to the other, brisk and efficient. Berenice pushed the punt out again, Mycroft pulled the girl on, Oona helped her and she sat in the bows wet and smiling and fair, the punt weighed down. Nicholas swung them with his pole over the black leaves of the lilies. The gold reached up to them, the reflection of gold leaves in still water. Nicholas pushed and they headed towards the island, the bubble house waiting.

It was so still, waiting, peaceful, expectant.

Plash.

A distant carillon, ringing happily, in no particular direction.

'Nobody about,' Berenice said, looking eagerly, side to side.

'Nobody is about almost everywhere here,' Mycroft said. He spoke very slowly, as if all his remarks welled up from some deep personal amusement. He was counting up the girl's backbone.

Nicholas remembered that they would find what they would find. It was sufficient for the true brother to know what he was doing, here and at this moment: to propel them across this water, to feel this pole within his hands. This too was the essential communication with that which was always present – so they were taught and so they believed and so could he experience.

The scent of the Community Bakery, the weight of the heat, welcome in winter, the carrying of trays of loaves, flour on the habit, the brusque face of Brother Michael, fingers touching dough. 'Feed my sheep.' Often Brother Nicholas had enjoyed that world, the same bricks, the same high monastic walls with the same single carved stone, as on all the buildings, the familiar, the carved twin fishes; and here also the bright heat under the ovens, the baking of bread, the sacrament in the silent monastery.

The coloured ducks kept them in convoy, bobbling in curiosity, a fleet of dons stately sailing on the gold. And then the island was about them, the house above them, the bright metallic stairway reaching down into the water before their bows. They could see veins of red in the milky walls, their eyes were led in among the semi-transparent textures. The house was too high, too large, to grasp as a single entity any more. The stairway vanished into golden water.

Berenice stood up in the bows and grabbed at it. Mycroft got out first so that he could help Oona, lifting himself heavily on to the metal steps. Berenice observed what was so obviously a familiar assistance, an enjoyment that his wife existed, an action done out of marriage rather than manners. There was a faint difference when he held the punt for her while she made fast. They both looked out towards her from their married state.

Her bare feet stood on the metal rungs of the ladder. Her toes grasped. She had to remember who she was. She was determined to be herself, Berenice without sentiment. . . . She was observing.

'It was all a pity,' Bruce had once said while he was drawing, 'that paintings cannot be so constructed that they flow.'

He had been drawing breasts, her breasts as she sat up, her breasts as she half turned away, her breasts as she lay back and their contour relaxed, subsided, retired a little into herself. The drawings were hard, real fiercely vivid Bruce drawings. She could remember the grey ceiling as she lay back on the musty cushion.

'Imagine Constable,' he had said unexpectedly. (Constable! Bruce!) 'Imagine Constable painting in Time – not painting the single instant. Not a film of things outside – but his direct thought and touch from his hand and mind. Imagine that he made a landscape twenty-four hours long, with all that bubble of water sounding, with his sunlight changing with the drift of a cloud on a Constable morning, with the sloshing of one of his horse's fetlocks in the shallow river. Imagine it commanding the attention that the single-instant canvas now receives, being looked at over and over again, being listened to. Imagine its sun rising, the whole thing turning in an endless circle, re-returning to its earlier morning. The cries of children going to school, their voices when they return, the call of an owl, the interrelation of colour and sound and form and mood. But seen through one mind. To be able to brush on a voice . . . the movement of a tree.'

The girl animal on the metal rungs of the ladder observing. The ducks still patrolled – an occasional dabble, the tall forest like a giant ballroom reaching in all directions. The little monk was carrying up her clothes. They went up the rungs together behind the Charringtons.

Their heads rose up to the level of the house. Their feet arrived on wooden decking. The bells, the carillon, had faded.

From where they stood the crystal-like walls curved upwards and they contained the clear plate windows, the huge windows, one covered a little with the yellow blossoms. It was difficult to decide whether there was one floor or three. But big as the windows were from where they stood they could not look into the house, they could only see reflections of themselves.

The door stood shut.

6

Mycroft was not awkward in any way.

'We will go in.' He spoke very evenly. (The unknown factor – one must be controlled to overcome natural unease.)

'Should we call first?' Nicholas suggested patiently.

'What about knocking?' Berenice asked over a tanned shoulder. Berenice was dressing while they decided. She could see herself in a window, somehow not particularly naked, not really peculiar for these peculiar circumstances. Bruce was always sad when it was time for her to dress. He did not get tired of drawing her, of touching her. Of course Bruce drew and touched and observed a seemingly endless circle of girls; often her own friends; once a coster's daughter he had found heaving a sack of spuds (a stringy rat-tailed physical girl), or another time a little school kid bribed with Coca-Cola and a Bruce smile. But he was always sad when he stopped drawing Berenice. While he drew her he was not silent as he so often was with the others, he would talk to her endlessly, he would make her lift up one hand so that he could just touch her under the arm, so that he could be certain that she was truly there. He would make her stand and sit and lie with a ruthless, endless, demanding self-interest. Now, by herself, he could not watch her dress. It was so warm. She was damp. With a grimace she pulled down her sweater over her head.

At that instant she saw, and saw so slowly, saw almost without alarm, what must be another figure reflected in the window and standing behind her. She could not see clearly, not through the sweater. She was unable, she could not, turn round or cry out. It was the figure of a child. And the others madly had not noticed, were knocking, were looking at the closed door, were not with her.

The sweater was on and Berenice forced herself to turn round. There was no one on the ladder, but she heard a flurry in the water. She darted to the edge of the platform but there was nothing to see – only the bright ducks in full retreat – why? But she could not be sure that she had seen anything.

'We must all keep together,' Mycroft was saying. She did not want to speak. She pulled at her skirt and zipped it up. It was gloriously warm. She stared out at the nervous paddling of the ducks. There was only that golden forest all empty.

'Coming,' Berenice said.

Brother Nicholas knew that he did not know what to expect and that this did not matter; there was a sufficiency of time. Each occurrence would appear at its appointed moment. He waited. They had knocked and they had paused and there had been no reply.

Brother Nicholas watched Mycroft. Coolly, considerately, with charity, one tried to place him within one's experience of men. Tall, he appeared to be diffident. The eyes moved over the scene before him as if the things that were perceived were not to be trusted, while the long fingers of the hands explored the texture of his own clothes as if there was a small uncertainty about their existence. They were hands that moved like crabs walking, as if they were feeling sideways.

That was the first impression.

But Nicholas was also noticing that Mycroft made his actual decisions like a measured clock. It was only in his reception of outside impressions that he exhibited such an elaborate caution. In action he proceeded from each considered move to each calculated conclusion. Nicholas watched the slow uncertain smile, the applied courtesy, the self-depreciation, and the precisely balanced determination.

He searches for the catch, the hands go clutchwise over the door.

There is no catch.

The door, it is a heavy door, is opened completely with a slow and deliberate push. He does not thrust at the door. It is always under control. He stops its movement with the direct grip of his hand.

Charrington stands firmly back. For a moment they wait.

There is no sound within the house. There is no chime of bells, no toll, no carillon, no distant tinkling high above. Almost, Brother Nicholas decided, they could hear their own breathing. He became very aware of his three companions: Mrs Charrington, magnificently collected, the piled black hair, the mature presence; Berenice dressed, casually, her hair still damp down her back, it was curious that he should now know this girl person; Mycroft Charrington, his weight on one foot, relaxed, the whole face watching.

They were assailed by the scents of new and unfamiliar woods, by the aromatic caress of spices on the senses.

'Wait,' Mycroft said.

They found themselves stock-still.

It was an open hall.

There were no floors above them. The roof, the inside of the bubble was a pattern of illumination, filtered, subdued, yet with a basic intensity of colour, an enormous elaboration, but stern. The shadows were calculated here. There seemed to begin, only a few feet above their heads, a space of decorated light. Yet also there were areas of darkness, areas surrounding an aperture, a recess of light shining. Transparencies projected walls of blues and greens. Beams of light seemed to form a criss-cross pattern, a web, a false ceiling above them beyond which there seemed to be a different, a disconnected, watching world.

But where they stood it was calm. Here it was pleasant, the new scents meandering in their nostrils.

'Look,' Oona said quietly. She moved to the centre, moving between the pools of light. Mycroft went forward with her.

Here was a polished refectory table, not large, flanked

63

by two chairs on either side. The table was laid for four, exaggerated Danish cutlery, grey stone-coloured plates, cold white linen and two large tureens, earthenware, plain, steaming gently as if they had only just been placed on their rush circular mats.

Berenice and Nicholas came round the table.

Beside each place was a piece of grey notepaper. The Monk picked one up and read:

'Doctor Oona Charrington.'

Mycroft's face twitched.

'You are sitting on this side, Brother Nicholas,' he said, looking at another place. 'We are expected. It seems that arrangements have been made.' The hands began again to make their sideways examination of himself.

There was a pause, a sense of isolation in the vast room.

'You are a doctor, Mrs Charrington?' Berenice broke in irrelevantly.

'Yes, I am a doctor,' Oona admitted. (One presents an immediate picture – one is given an immediate responsibility.)

They waited on in silence again.

Mycroft was still inspecting, methodically, continuously.

'We must explore the whole building . . . first,' he mused. 'We are not forbidden to explore. At this stage I am almost certain that we shall find nothing. But we must look, we must try to find some inkling of what and where we are. I do not think that we shall become more certain, but I think we must make the attempt.'

Nicholas was nodding his partial agreement.

64

'Yes, perhaps we should all walk round this building together. But it is also evident that we are guests here; that this place, this meeting, is intended. I was thinking that perhaps we should – accept the invitation – and sit down. Yet I agree, perhaps we ought to look round first.'

Almost imperceptibly the pools of colour changed in tone, merging, brightening, dying away, with the slow imperturbability of the hour hand of a clock.

'We are still ourselves,' Oona reminded them. 'We don't owe anybody any allegiance for being here. It was not our choice. We have just been kidnapped.'

'Is this perhaps – an experiment?' Mycroft suggested. 'We have been isolated here to prove something maybe.'

It was Berenice who made the counter-suggestion.

'I remember being told that it was an emergency.'

'Your emergency, our emergency, we four?'

'We don't know,' Berenice reminded him.

She followed them as they turned to examine the building. She glanced back once at the steaming tureens. Swimming had brought an appetite. She also remembered what she thought she had seen. Somehow she did not want to mention it. The building was extraordinary.

The building was only one room, it seemed. There was no kitchen, no bathroom, no other room at all. In the centre there was this table with four chairs, with the meal laid and waiting.

At the right-hand end they found a tiled area: soft

green-blue rippling tiles about a small pool with dappled fish, with a tiny rockery and delicate white flowers growing between the stones. There were grey comfortable chairs about it, set as if for conversation, each with a small attendant table. Oona noted that there were exactly four of these easychairs and that two of them had been placed close together, side by side. There were no notes on the chairs, but the two together had cushions decorated with the white shapes of swans in flight. The third chair had a bright cushion, the rising sun in brilliant orange rays. The fourth chair was without any kind of cushion at all.

There seemed to be no other doors, only the entrance.

At the other end of the house (almost, Nicholas decided afterwards, he had expected it) four simple beds were lined up as if within a dormitory. They were already made up, with plain grey rugs and cream fresh sheets. Two beds were side by side, the other two a little farther apart.

Above the beds, above the grey chairs and the rockery, above the refectory table and the waiting meal was the dome alight with the muted colours of nacarat and plum; the inner side of the glass bubble.

Outside, through the huge windows – the artificial forest.

Oona was looking at Mycroft.

'We are the mice,' she endorsed.

'The stage is set,' Mycroft began.

'I think,' Nicholas suggested patiently, 'that we must begin by accepting this invitation.'

They walked back, unspeaking, to the dining-table.
'Food,' Berenice thought.

The grey notes ordained that Oona should sit opposite
her husband. She approved at once of their host. She liked
to sit opposite Mycroft over food, to talk to him directly.
It was good to see his mouth form words. She liked his
approval of the flair of her suit, the feel of her own teeth
on a nut he had cracked for her, the courtesy that would
reach out of his intertwining thinking and support her
in a conversation with strangers, his aplomb in the em-
barrassing situation. One's suspenders could snap; one's
bag, with the theatre tickets, could be left at home; one's
cheque-book could still be on the plane; Mycroft was
still glad to have you here.

One serves this unexpected dinner. One has always
served dinner, the same deft and considered movements
as one makes in the casualty surgery, Mycroft waiting,
lean and hungry, bean-shoots, noodles, chicken and soy
sauce. Chinese food is wonderful and there are second
helpings, everybody is eating. And now – one delights in
maintenance, the perpetual and satisfying motions of
continuing. It is like preparing breakfast or the firm
closing of one's own heavy curtains, or writing the tidy
prescription for a favourite old lady's arthritis or the
familiar list of wants from the family grocer. Maintenance!
That certainty of knowing what to do, the voice giving
confidence to the old man dying in the small back bed-
room (death too is a form of maintenance, often unrecognized but nevertheless essential) holding his hand

firmly, checking his pulse, but more important the feel of one's hand on his old hand, time for his death, there was to be no hurry, he was entitled to it. Or there was that girl who had her baby on the self-service shop floor, well she wasn't Oona's patient but of course these things occur, delivery on a brand new copy of the *Daily Express*. The startled grocer and the girl's flesh heaving; birth between the aisles tall with cereals and offers of custard powder. A perfectly natural process. ('Quite a lady,' the grocer said. Well she was being a lady now all right.) A seven and a half pound boy to the Hon. Phoebe Maitland, all ship-shape and Bristol fashion and the girl exhausted. Mycroft would probably insist on presenting a christening mug. Mycroft would.

'More, Brother Nicholas?'

One watched Nicholas smile and refuse although he enjoyed – moderation, control and patience. Discipline has a good taste when it is mastered.

Berenice grinned and no she had better not have any more and Mycroft of course did. He had the large appetite of the scrawny, of the man with curiosity.

And she looked up. Oona did not know why. There above them, above where they sat, were the lighted patterns, the domes illuminated, the deliberate shadows. A child was sitting in a bright recess looking down at her, a girl not yet fourteen, a girl in a pleated skirt, a tartan in pale blues. It was watching the eaters below and their eyes met. Its fingers were at once lifted to its lips in a commanding easy admonition, as if she and Oona were in league, and Oona looked away. Absurdly the others had not seen and did not know. Again she looked up. It had disappeared. It had been there. The recess was empty.

Oona continued with her eating. She did not want any more noodles. She did not speak.

Down here they were eating normally.

It was after the meal. They had . . . nothing to do. There was nowhere to explore. Their needs were satisfied. They all sat, the chairs had been provided. Nicholas was sitting in the chair without the cushion.

On a window-sill there was a jug of coffee – cups. They had all looked outside. There was nobody to be seen, only the round lake, the jade trunks of the trees leading in every direction. It was evident that the coffee was there to be drunk, to be enjoyed, not an excuse to begin a wild-goose chase. The cups, they had not noticed the cups before, were satisfying. Perhaps the shape, the texture, the colour of the blue-grey glaze, the way the handle fitted to the finger. It was a long time since Brother Nicholas had drunk coffee, seated in a comfortable chair.

They were at ease, suddenly looking at each other, at themselves as 'four-people', as the now normal anchor of their present existence.

And now what do we do? Nicholas asked himself.

'Now what do we do?' Brother Nicholas asked the assembled company, and he watched them while they were considering.

'It is a quiet emergency,' Mycroft suggested. While he was explaining he sat absolutely still. 'Everything that we have done has been arranged for, we were expected, we were fed, we are at rest. No doubt the next stage will soon arrive. Perhaps the crisis, the nub of the matter, will then be disclosed. We don't know. But at least another stage will appear. I am quite certain of this. These – elaborate preparations, they have not been made for nothing.'

'I am sure you are right,' the monk was agreeing. 'In the meantime we can only wait.'

Oona spoke quietly, not with any note of irritation, almost like passing a remark about the weather.

'I'm tired of waiting. I know that there must be some sort of answer, but will it be an answer that we are going to enjoy?'

'I still think that this is an emergency,' Berenice said.

'Our emergency,' Mycroft insisted. 'We can only suffer our own emergencies.'

They paused, sat silently, as if they were all consciously waiting.

Waiting, Brother Nicholas mused, waiting was also service, waiting was often service. To wait, as the aged Prior was never impatient of reminding him, was to live. To take a human life was a sin of considerable magnitude. Also one did not waste a human life, and one had an especial responsibility towards one's own. 'We are here. Let us not forget to be here. We must see to it that by the end we have *been*.' And Nicholas himself had reminded others, while he had been the novice master: 'Life here in the Community is restricted, we know that it has set bounds, that it knows firstly simplicity. But within that simplicity – remember that it is also free, free of complication, you are free to be your true selves, to be most clear both to your brothers and to your own eyes. This self must not only be sacrificed to the Community, sloughed off so that you may plainly see it for what it is, this self must also in the truest sense be *given*. There must be a self to give.'

The young men gathered before him, six shorn heads in the echoing library with the carved twin fishes, and these novices had, it seemed, been with him a long time, and he smiled and led them out into the garden for a few minutes. The long wall and the two laburnum trees and a thrush hopping. There they must stand, each alone with himself and in silence. The call of the Abbey bell will sound across the island. All things and all times gathered here together in one place and at one moment.

Confitemini Domino quoniam bonus.

And also, Nicholas remembered, the brisk attention of baking bread, making shoes and helping a cow to calve and the blue Virgin hanging in the cow barn and the rustle and the tang of hay. And now catapulted unexpectedly back into (or out of) the world. Yet here not into activity but comfort and a patient idleness. Comfort, a mild luxury, leisure; these things too, now and in their place, were a stern, a particularly real challenge.

The others were talking, and he found – he knew that he was paying no attention. He gazed out and through the window.

Comfort and joy were not to be conquered by flight. These things must be endured.

He stretched out his sandalled feet over the grey and greening tiles towards the pool. The silver spotted fish hung below him in their own dimensions, making their way between weeds and through artificial stone places, and they were not knowing him.

Somebody, Nicholas reflected, must feed them. He looked up and outward, out through one of the huge picture windows, out into the still copper-coloured wood beyond them, the light unchanging, the elegant rising pillars, the hanging cascades of metal golden leaves. He was not, he thought, drunk with this place just now, he was not captivated, or perhaps this was an illusion while he sat so still. But he was hearing the bells again or rather now a single bell striking slowly, sonorously, a single note tolling and waiting in his ear. He saw his own walking earlier that day – morning? afternoon? He did not know – it had been like walking through curtains of flowers, he was parting and parting them with his hands. Outside, outside through the window, he could see a child standing on the decking, kilted in blue with short black hair and she was looking in his direction, not with any surprise but with a steady weighing intelligence, her arms akimbo, her feet slightly apart. He realized, after the first moment of recognition, that it was indeed himself with which she seemed to be concerned and for an instant he felt himself to be an insect imprisoned in hopeless cotton wool at the bottom of a test-tube. But the monk did not move. It was ridiculous that his companions did not seem to see her, but they were not looking and he found that there was no temptation to point her out, only to remain still, to watch this searching observation of himself. And she was not there. Even as he pondered she disappeared. The dappled fish continued to swim at his feet. The chair and the comfort remained.

Nemo beatus nisi justus.

Now this, Mycroft Charrington considered, should be the ending of one stage of the process. He did not know of course, it was an inspired guess, but science throughout its history has been a regular and unforseeable series of inspired irrational guesses. If certain recurrences repeat themselves sufficiently often before our rather limited means of perception, then what we call a great truth has been exposed, a new monolith has been upraised . . . until the moment when that little man at the back of the hall points out, demonstrates, explains, that your great pattern is not, is not quite what we thought. Presto! The quicksands are always waiting.

But, always, Mycroft used to remind himself while watching his students, science is for persons. These ideas are for actual men to think about, and they are our eyes that watch the pointer on the dial, the scales, the punched tape and the typed figures that disclose an answer, for our fascination, for our rejoicing and for our despair. We wonder, as we sip our coffee that somebody else has thoughtfully provided (both here and at the laboratory), we wonder if somebody else has solved our conundrum. We wonder how much will be understood even if we do manage to come out first with some sort of answer. We speculate, forgetting that this is not the end product. So many people make the mistake of thinking that we are going somewhere, like passengers in a jet liner, with a hostess serving and smiling – bottle of tax free gin, sir? – touch-down at Amsterdam in ten minutes. Science is a flight without a landing. It is our own selves each day that we are making. Science is not out there as we sit in our cool white coats, but here under the hair that we ought to have combed and is now upstanding. It will be good to see Oona in the evening, it will be a good evening without appointment or distraction but simply to go home, to the doctor's house with the comfortable furniture. He had his own desk set in the huge bay of the vast Victorian room, set with his back to the curtains so that he could see his wife reading by the tall bookshelves in a pool of warm light and the telephone within reach of her hand. He made diagrams on his desk, diagrams that his students would never see, that were devised in his own private method of notation – his own particular ideas. If certain recurrences repeat themselves sufficiently often. . . . When she had her duty nights he did not make love to her. Sometimes he would love her unexpectedly, before the roaring fire in her own surgery downstairs, or he had made her happy against the tiled wall of their own small kitchen. He liked to see her. Now he sat at his desk with his papers (playing with his diagrams she called it, with her understanding smile – for she knew the key to his diagrams) . . . and then the phone would ring and she would go and Mycroft would be restless. He would fill the thermos with hot milk against her late return, he would go upstairs and close the curtains, take off the bedcover, prowl, thinking his own thoughts but unanchored while she was not there. He would have particularly good ideas with one ear cocked for the Jaguar's return, her book still open and upside-down on her empty chair.

So many times – when Geoffrey was at home during the school holidays, his son drinking milk last thing, a gloriously warm evening in high summer, the boy in his pyjama trousers. (At his school it was not done to wear the top.) Geoffrey always so brown like his mother, almost burnt black in the summer.

'I wish Mummy wasn't always away in the evenings.'

'She has a sense of duty, Geoffrey.'

Now to sit here and together in this calculated and extraordinary house. Oona sat here as always, capable and waiting and oddly at peace in the uncertainty. For the present she could not offer him herself, or herself walking with Geoffrey, or Geoffrey in the bath talking physics with his father. She sat patiently.

A pair of bare feet were now walking into the house out of the golden light outside. A young person, with short black hair, in a very short pleated blue skirt buckled at the hip and a white shirt had joined them. It was really only a child. It came with a quiet confident purpose. Everyone could see it, nobody seemed surprised, which was absurd, not even Oona was surprised. It stood in front of Mycroft.

'Good evening,' it said.

The next stage in the process had begun.

75

7

'Good evening,' it said.

The hair was cropped close to the head and there were dark eyes and a cool face; at moments there were doubts that it was a girl. A certain almost indefinable roundness in the limbs convinced Doctor Charrington – but the girl was very spare and its muscles were hard.

It stood absolutely still.

The build was that of a child perhaps, that moment in the act of leaving childhood – but it did not quite seem to be in the time of childhood. The face, the texture of the skin, they were young. But there was also the glance, the way its figure stood with an accustomed authority, there was a look of powerful waiting confidence as it stood before them in the glowing light, arms folded, eyes watching.

Oona felt curiously uncertain.

They all moved forward in their chairs, in interest, in surprise, suddenly jerked out of a false half normality. It was the monk who spoke first. He had perhaps an advantage over the others. It was for him a little easier to call upon his certainties.

'Who are you?' he asked.

It did not move.

Then:

'Good evening,' it said again.

It stood there, feet slightly apart, bare feet on the tiles and now it was not looking at them directly. It spoke as if it was repeating some sort of formal lesson.

'I think that you will have to find out who I am – in your own way. Each one of you will have to discover your own individual mode of comprehension.'

Mycroft watched it make this exposition and then he saw it change. He saw it remember to change as it walked forward, for it scratched its thigh, allowed itself to be distracted, stopped to look down at its fishes and then knelt down and sat back on its heels. It showed them that this place belonged to it. Mycroft Charrington, his wife, Berenice and the monk, they were all at once made its guests. It dabbled a finger in the water.

'Suppose you just assume that for the moment I am the competent authority.' It screwed up its nose and looked round at them. It grinned.

There was a waiting pause. They did not know how to answer. Oona found herself noticing that it possessed an extra pair of pointed dog teeth.

'And did you eat well?' The dark eyes looked from one to the other of them with amusement.

But Brother Nicholas was not to be deflected.

'Why have we been brought here?' he continued.

It laughed and turned back to its fishes. It had a deep laugh for a child.

'To try our food,' it suggested. Berenice had a view of the soles of its feet as it lay flat on its tummy as if to look even more closely at the water. It was evident that it wore nothing under its kilt.

'We did enjoy your dinner,' Mycroft stated evenly. It was a first offering. 'But I think that we are entitled to know why we have been brought here – to know what it is all about.'

His fingers were folding together – waiting.

It was busy.

'We have been kidnapped,' Oona pointed out. 'We did not ask to come here.'

'No,' it agreed. The white hand was darting down, teasing the fishes. It leaned out to reach to the centre of the pool.

'It is a natural curiosity,' Mycroft began to insist. The creature did not seem to be taking too much notice. It grunted.

Berenice sat watching the movements of the long and faintly gawky adolescent limbs. She sat in this comfortable chair, drawing a girl in her mind, drawing her prone by a tiled pool. She did not include the transparent house round it, quite deliberately. She did not include the extraordinary parkland beyond the high windows. Bruce would have wasted time trying to do that.

Oona was trying again for them all.

'Why are *you* here?' she asked. Oona hardly looked at it while she spoke. She was arriving at certain opinions.

It paid her immediate attention. It was on its feet and

it was above them. Oona found that it had come to her –
not playing now – purposeful.

'Tell me – grip my hand – would you say that I am real –
do you think that I am here?' The voice was almost too
deep, a liquid dark compelling experienced voice.
'Examine me, Doctor Charrington.'

It knew their names. Perhaps it was obvious that it
should know their names.

The elder woman leaned forward out of her armchair.
'Very well.'

Oona was unflurried. Here was a moment of question,
an accustomed professional situation, a chance to satisfy
her own immediate curiosity.

She gripped its hands. They were warm. She felt for
the pulse. It was stolidly regular. She made it kneel. It
was looking her straight in the eye and Oona stared back.
It had to open its mouth, have an ear inspected, feel its
eyelid pulled back. Doctor Charrington made it stand
up while she glanced at the length of its legs. It had to
back towards the others while she lifted the hem of its
kilt. It did not flinch in any way. It was a girl, a fluff
of new dark hair between its legs. Oona felt it as if it
was a horse at a fair. It ought to flinch if it were touched –
so. It had to unbuckle the kilt, the shirt had to be undone.
A stray black hair or so pointed up towards a soft girl's
navel. Oona touched it with a finger. The breasts under
its shirt were only just defined, were beginning to grow.
It was observed that there were no marks, no moles, no
freckles, no spots or scars.

'You are here,' Oona admitted. 'Got up to look about

twelve and a half or thirteen. I would say that you function. You eat, drink, make water, defecate and sleep. Being a consultant to a children's hospital I would hazard the guess that you have been having monthly periods for about a year. You are quite perfect. Medically speaking you are certainly present as an early adolescent. But I think that this is quite irrelevant to what you are. I cannot claim to be more than a second-class botanist but I do know – they are not trees outside that window. They only look like trees. Don't they?'

It nodded, looking very serious.

'I think they are trees,' it said. 'For my purposes, just at the moment, they are trees. They may as well be trees.'

It straightened and smoothed its kilt. It was very like a girl.

(Doctor Charrington checked off the points in her mind that she had not disclosed: an extra pair of teeth, the quality of the voice, the muscles more reminiscent of a sixteen-year-old boy, nothing so particularly unusual.)

'I don't think you are real.'

Mycroft heard Berenice say it. He saw that Berenice had shaken out her fair hair and was now standing as if to gain some point of vantage over their – hostess. Berenice was so undoubtedly full-grown. She was smiling at the creature, as if already there was some secret that they shared.

'I don't believe that you are real in the way you are trying to convince us. We can touch you and see you and hear you and all the rest of it. But there is something else. I have been looking at you. There is something not quite complete. There is something more in your design. I want to look at you, can I perhaps look at you – in my way?'

It glanced up for a moment from its thinking. It was evidently not put out, not surprised, at what was being said to it, it was only savouring what it had heard. It wiped its nose with the back of its brown hand. It looked up at Berenice direct.

'I've seen inside your portfolio. You left it outside. I've seen all the stuff at your place in the Gloucester Road. I was the last to see it. You make things belong to you, don't you, Berenice. Everything that you see – that's your way of seeing it, isn't it? You are unable to look in any other way.' It grinned. 'How will you look at me?'

Berenice remembered Mr Eriksson earlier, he had seen what she had put on paper, his twisted fingers had turned the sheets, had looked up with a different interest at the person behind the marks and lines at which he had been staring.

Berenice looked away from the creature, looked away over the whole extent of the house, over the green-tiled floor and over the refectory table and up and out through the picture-windows to the forest and up higher to the brilliant interior of the patterned domes curving over them. She looked anywhere but at where it was standing awaiting her answer.

Berenice looked back to the floor again. She remained

firm. She just pointed to a spot in the centre of the house beneath the dome.

'First – you must go and stand just there.'

Mycroft was asking himself what she was trying to do.

'Stand still, with your face towards us and your hands on your hips and your feet a little apart. Keep your eyes closed. You must not look at us.'

Oona had seen it glance at Berenice and had watched it pad barefoot to the spot she had indicated. At moments, when it moved it still did not look like a girl. It stood just as and where it had been told, its feet a little apart.

Berenice too was still standing, standing very tall, was looking at the creature very intently.

Nicholas suddenly realized that Berenice was cautioning him, was cautioning all of them.

'Now don't just look at her. Try and look up and around her – do you see the pools of colour projected by the dome, the yellow and the orange, the pattern of the tiles about her feet? Just relax your looking. Just keep her figure within your line of vision. Expect nothing. Watch patiently. Then I think you will see the complete design.'

For an instant only Doctor Charrington saw – and lost. It was as if the creature was magnified, projected upwards so that it was for a single moment vast, a living torso reaching high into the dome, its own eyes closed and sightless, while an owl outstretched, befeathering its loins, benignly stared . . . and was gone.

The creature was speaking quite calmly. There it was,

hands on hips, standing where it had been asked in its blue kilt, the brown eyes now open.

'Have you seen in the way you wanted, Berenice Elm?'

Berenice nodded. She would make no comment, she was drawing in her mind, it was sufficient to see.

It was Nicholas who walked round to the other side. He looked at the creature quietly and without hurry. He would say, in his description, that he was not certain, that he was only certain that in its position, as Berenice had placed it, it was a work of art. He would say that it had a looking of powerful, waiting confidence that could destroy the distance into which it stared. It was as if something was about to happen.

He took out his black-covered notebook. He had made an entry earlier in the day.

It dawned on Mycroft, as he sat forward in his chair, what it was that Berenice did. It had been at once a physical organization of colours and lights that became patterns – colours and lights to the perceptions, patterns recognized by the mind. At the same time these patterns had circled around the creature which in its turn simultaneously evoked emotions and memories of previous emotions, thoughts and perceptions until the whole thing jumped forward in one intuitive leap; it composed itself into one unique and unexpected juxtaposition – a new experience.

In research though there is always that perpetual open question. Every day, every evening, he would come down the steps of the laboratory building, either baffled because he could not find an answer, or sometimes excited because he was asking a new question. The delight in the itch on the mind's skin!

The creature had turned round, it was looking back at them, its nose puckered with amusement. It ran back towards them and did a cartwheel in front of Brother Nicholas.

'Now that you have looked at me, in your way, what do you see? Do you think that I'm here? Do you think that something is here? Do you ask yourself what I am?'

It sat down, all flushed from its exertions and exuberance at their feet.

'I can understand what you are,' Brother Nicholas replied.

Suddenly Nicholas knew himself to be at ease, he had remembered his own peace, he was taking his novices across the rock-hewn garden, sheltered here from the wind but within sound of the sea. There had been time. He had broken off from his dissertation and they had been led out here and they had stood still and had listened. Here was today! As Father Prior had said, had explained, had reminded: 'One must reach beyond explanation and keep silent.' How often had the Prior himself sat motionless behind his ancient desk – interview by presence rather than by conversation. For these moments Nicholas was silent with himself. This new place too had peace, the still and artificial forest, the motionless green and golden water aglow beyond the windows, the occasional note now of a solitary bell. Where he was, here and at this place, was becoming familiar. He had himself, that was luggage enough. He looked at his questioner as it sat at his feet panting like a small and eager dog. He knew his own authority.

'You are what they used to call a Goddess,' he said.

He was not excited. He took his time.

'You see, I have an understanding of these things. Even in my religion, and sometimes we admit it, there can only be a half answer. We can only ever explain in terms of our restricted knowledge, our narrow experience. The treasure that is mankind consists of only quite small change. No religion can go beyond the capacity of the minds with which we have been endowed. We can only grasp with such equipment as we may have. A rational idea is only a key that happens to fit the very limited pattern of our minds.

'The old Gods, they were yet another conception, a differing experience to my present faith, of the still same reality. Of this great reality, of this so much greater, more ramified, more complex and yet perhaps simpler capacity that lies behind the old Gods, behind my faith, behind yourself, we see only a minute segment. But the value of our very small change, that does not alter, small though it may be. To the extent of my understanding my religion is true. To the extent of my understanding and no further, you exist.'

It had tucked its heels under its bottom. Oona saw that it had a pocket in its skirt which it was exploring. It threw out a London bus ticket, found a hankie and began to pick its nose.

There was a pause.

'Aren't you afraid of me?' it asked.

85

Nicholas both nodded and shook his head.

'Yes and no. That is because there is another side to this small minted coin. You see I am a man and man is so powerful by comparison with what he knows. In men the Gods commit the terrible crimes of which they themselves are quite incapable. In men they taste the exquisite trembling delights too fragile for the immortal touch. For only a man, by reason of his pre-set limitations, can experience the actual meaning of your creation. In that we are greater than you, we are the more powerful. For we have been granted the essential weakness, the necessary ignorance to experience both value and taboo. Thus only for man is a true heaven possible. Only through us is your experience known. That is why you fashion this our brief mortality, holding all our birth, our life, our death, in your hand. That is why you sit there as a human, not as a disembodied ghost . . . Man is a frightful lovely thing. Only in our guise can you, omnipotent and omnipresent, yet fully understand. But only in your totality can we, small and stupid as we are, experience your uttermost and unlimited mercy, and so survive.'

It had found a sweet in its pocket. It was sucking it slowly, sucking and thinking.

It nodded.

It waited.

It spoke quite slowly.

'What is your opinion, Mr Charrington? I am medically present, a place in a design, a Goddess – have you got a suggestion? You have got some ideas, haven't you?'

Mycroft's long legs moved outwards from his chair as

he sprawled back. Oona was amused by his so characteristic motion. He liked children. It was obvious to Oona that he had already weighed the various possibilities, that he was moving on to questions rather than to any conclusion. His hands were not walking. He was at peace.

'I would judge you,' Mycroft said to it, kindly and deliberately, 'with the rest of this place. You seem to me to be a portion of it. It was all intended to produce a certain effect, yourself included. I do not propose to consider you *in vacuo* as it were. You know what I mean. You are asking us whether we believe in your existence – for a reason. There is a reason for us to be here. So, provisionally, in light of the existing evidence and until I receive some contrary information, this is a matter that I must keep open. But as a working hypothesis, and research cannot continue without the imaginative framework of the working hypothesis . . .'

He stopped and grinned at it.

'I will believe in you.'

It was up, it was jumping to its feet. Suddenly it was enthusiastic. It was no longer waiting.

'So I am here,' it announced triumphantly.

It held up its hand. It demanded attention. It could not be gainsaid.

'You must come out on to the deck. It is easier there.'

They found themselves following.

They had left their comfortable chairs, the relaxed sense of unmoving comfort, they were trooping out like a collection of children.

Outside, for the first time, there was a movement in the air, the sudden relief of an unexpected breeze. Berenice was very conscious of scents, sharp flavours touching the inside of her nose, coming to her from the forest. Berenice wondered if it was her imagination but the yellow light above them seemed to have been softened by a degree, to have lost some of its intensity. Did they have evening here? Night? What time was it? There was a refreshingly joyous warmth. She could feel herself standing still, her feet on the wood, her body all the way up, fed and satisfied, a strand of her own fair hair just in the sight of her left eye. There were those painted ducks, dabbling and voyaging.

Queerk! So comfortable.

They were outside their own house, Mr and Mrs Charrington, Brother Nicholas, herself – it was their house. Their chairs, their beds, the place where they had eaten. Here, she, Berenice was physically present.

There it was, sitting astried the rail, its legs dangling.

Oona felt oddly aware that here, at last, there could no longer be any outside communications; only Mycroft, these friends. She was able to concentrate on the present moment, on Mycroft standing, watching, waiting, without hurry. There were no household commitments, the note for the milk, the extra milk and the extra coffees for Mycroft's colleagues. There was no compulsive need to read the unwanted literature from glossy commercial firms about improbable drugs – the note-taking which her in-built sense of professionalism insisted that she must always continue.

It was looking across the water, away from them, its legs swinging, the hair on the back of its neck crisp with recent cropping.

Brother Nicholas was accustomed, not overawed, by the sense of quiet, the gentle movement of distant branches, the unhurried falling light. . . . Yet he felt himself to be outside his own framework and almost automatically his mind began to reassemble that framework about him, the ordered genuflexions of thought, the unvoiced singing to his God, the trickle of prayer that was usual to his mind. He was aware that his God did not require these actions, that these continual calls and praises were not needed 'up there', but were needed by the little human struggling to keep his solitary bridge open, struggling to remain in contact with the real instead of the daily dreaming of the foolish physical world.

Mycroft stood motionless now, emptying his mind, draining it of possibilities, only alert, only waiting for what was to be heard. His mind still held the network of his theories but they were unattended for the present, exhibits in a closed museum where the lights had been extinguished. Only the value remained. He waited to pounce on ideas.

'Upstairs,' it said. It was looking out across the lake water.

'Upstairs,' it said again, 'at about the time you came down here – there was the expected emergency. You'll not be surprised at its happening. You'll only be surprised that it has happened, in its way, to you. You'll only be surprised that it has happened now. It was never going to happen "now". The preparations had been made – you all knew that, vaguely. There was a cold decision. Now it has happened. The attackers – you have destroyed them too; your system worked, the great retaliation. (Or were they retaliating against you?) In each case – there has only been a success. For them as well the particular moment has arrived. It is no comfort to London that they are dead, no comfort to them that London is dying. Only the absurdity . . .'

It sat musing – and they listened, they did not interrupt it. It scratched itself under an arm. It looked at them, one to the other, the legs swinging.

'I had the best view. It was like a big red sun over Westminster Abbey for a whole detectable instant – the opening of a furnace door, not just in the face, it undressed you. For some only the sound came afterwards, even after the ear-drums were broken, the sound in the head. The City Brokers, they knew nothing about it. The City is not far from Westminster. But one City man, from beyond Hampstead, had left his house quite late. His wife had been unwell, she was a little better. He was by a wall and that sun could just shine over it and his bowler was burnt into his head. One hundred miles away the blast was still travelling, curiously, unpredictably, shapes and hulks where houses were. In the final moments it was difficult to grasp, to understand what it was all about. Just before dying it was possible for a woman to see her husband lying supine in the grass and smiling and the smile getting broader, the smile that was John's blood coming slowly from the corner of his mouth. Three men in one row were fired into a patterned glaze on the vitreous china of a now public urinal. A woman emerged from a deep basement after an hour, the body alive, the mind quite dead and loudly screaming. But for the great majority – nothing. For most of those that were left – the pain did not continue for very long. It was time for me to come downstairs – and meet you here.'

It stopped.

The distant carillon of bells sounded joyfully through the fading tree-tops, coming closer, becoming almost deafening before passing away again.

They heard its voice pronounce words:

'You and I, we are not concerned with what has happened for we have another yet more searching problem still.'

8

There were two other aspects of its behaviour that convinced Oona Charrington that her original diagnosis
was sound. The first was its evident and effective authority
– its charisma as it were.

They had gone to bed like sheep. They were now sitting
up like overgrown children in an overgrown nursery. It
brought them something unrecognizable to drink, green
and sparkling in stone wine cups that was not wine. The
liquid was a powerfully efficient antidote to their sense
of shock, the stored shock of the whole day's experiences.
The drink was in no way sedative – they were already
tired – nor yet a stimulant. There was, Oona reflected,
simply a sense of restoration. They could lie in bed at
peace. And bed was good.

Secondly there was this sense of an enormous thankful-
ness, this release from responsibility. The creature, in its
patient understanding of their minds, was no child,
only the energy of a child's body at play – the expertise,
the actual authority and care, this was something that
she could recognize. It folded up their clothes, straightened up their blankets, they were warm, relaxed, at peace,
because this had never been a child.

The inevitable question was asked:

'Why are we here?' Berenice began.

'Why were you born? That's another question that we don't get answered,' it said, plumping up her pillows.

They all lay back patiently thinking about the day. The light beyond the windows had gone but in here the house was still illuminated though they could not quite see how. They remained intoxicated with a level pleasing sanity.

Brother Nicholas observed the accepted intimacy of their situation. They had gone to bed as bidden, the four pairs of pyjamas fitted, there was an emblem of twin fishes on his pocket. There was Oona Charrington, she had a dark skin; he had seen Berenice again, he had not tried even then through his own distress to look away. His Confessor had once said to him – he had come across a girl joyously sunbathing on the island, he had been in the course of his duties: 'The desire, my son, is a necessary gift for the continuation of life, for the delight in living. Not the desire but the use put to that emotion is the true test that you must give yourself.' And his Confessor had been elected Prior.

And now:

The shattered desk without a chair, the uncloistered abbey. The novice class? The scattered garden? To lie in bed, to receive the comfort of sleep. Lord have mercy upon them, Christ have mercy upon them, Lord have mercy upon them. He was the brotherhood – and he must sleep.

Mycroft looked upwards, at the mysterious and darkening patterns of the house, of the bubble, the vanishing shadowing colours, the gloom in each blackening recess. He tasted the greenly sparkling liquid on his tongue, he was helpless before the growing steady well-being within.

It was unusual to see Oona sleeping so far away from himself. He remembered that girl medical student on that first glorious Sunday morning, waking him with tea in her bachelor flat, the two cups unmatching and Oona laughing. He remembered opening and shutting his eyes as he lay there, telling himself that it was not true, testing that she was real and Oona every time he reopened them.

He closed his eyes.

It waited – it waited until they were all sleeping. The expression drained from the face, it gazed sphinx-like, engraved over the sleepers. Once it looked closely at Berenice, the fair girl's knees were bunched up high, a hand tight between her thighs, totally unconscious. Then it turned, padded silently to the outside door and opened it quietly. As it left the light fell dim.

Outside there came the beating of huge wings.

9

And it was a true morning.

Brother Nicholas awoke not believing in yesterday until he opened his eyes, not even then grasping the reality of the transparent house about him, the bright definition of pattern and light above his head. To one side, there lay Mycroft, a shock of dark frizzy hair on the cream-coloured pillow, one arm thrust up, the face asleep. The monk turned once. Berenice, on the other side, was a mound under the blanket, a mass of fair hair on the sheet.

The monk got up.

Taking his habit and his sandals he trotted to the door and slipped outside. The colours, the interior glory of the house was intruding upon him. Outside the air was newly fresh, the light serene, a quiet subdued nobility. He stopped. Now for the first time since he had taken that first walk from the lift and had arrived at the lakeside – he was alone. It was wonderful to stand still. The jade-like trees stretched away across the lake water in all directions, there were endless vistas up diverging avenues. Suddenly, a long way away he could make out a group of small white deer gliding, it seemed, above the ground, sleek coats in spotted browns. They were too far distant for him to hear their movement. Slowly he walked along the deck about the transparent house.

From the far end the land appeared to rise, further still quite steeply – a climbing forest with an avenue like a great greening copper staircase. Close to the shore there were figures moving among the trees, carrying loads away from him and running, but they seemed to be children; more were in the water, he could see heads above the surface, swimmers between the floating lily pads, swimming round the pillars. Nicholas felt them to be children only in the sense that last night's visitor was a child.

He knew with certainty now and here that they would not acknowledge him, he did not signal, he regarded them as figures in a landscape. His attention was distracted by what he thought might be a bird but as it came nearer he realized that it was in fact a great bat, a bat not flapping but hanging on the air with silver wings and all the majesty of a gull, a round black furry face, benign and calm, it banked across the lake, sliding through the arches and sailing away from him between the rising trees.

Standing between the clear windows he re-donned his familiar habit and remembered who he was. Familiar words jostled his mind for release, came gladly to him for their abiding certainty:

To pray in silence . . .

His voice said:

'Let them praise the name of the Lord, for he commanded and they were created. And he established them for ever and ever: he gave a decree which shall not pass away.'

The others were still asleep.

He picked up those pyjamas. He would walk round the house, right round – the words of the morning office came to his lips without sound, his eyes saw the brothers in their lines in the high Abbey church, the men's low voices lifting their litany with a patient splendid happiness like the waves of the sea . . .

. . . Brother John, Brother Bernard, Brother Geofric, Brother Francis, Brother Thomas, Brother Ulric, Brother Luc –

– their faces looked at by a great red sun

– rubble and the garden rocks with burnt flowers.

He stopped still, not wanting to remember.

It was lying under a curve of the turbid multi-coloured glass, stretched out in an abandoned comfort under the golden sky, quite naked, its kilt tucked under its head. It was fast asleep and Nicholas was almost falling over it.

It stayed apparently fast asleep as he stood there, half formed, neither child nor woman, a kind of level honey colour all over its body, its hands tucked over its small breasts, as unself-conscious as a puppy. It was as if it was in keeping with this place – as if someone was touching some button the eyelids were pulling open and it was looking up at him and the lips smiled.

'Hello,' it was saying, and it was a kind of explosive enthusiasm and it was putting up a hand to be helped and Nicholas found that he had to reach down to help it. It was warm to his touch, it was kissing him like a dog and standing against him and his hands were touching it and it was a beautiful and a perfect animal. Then he realized that it was standing quite still and watching him, it liked him, an amused vanity came into its face. Then it sprang away and up on to the balustrade and it was running along it and off it and then it was skipping back to him.

'Mornings, mornings, hurrah for mornings.'

It was shouting, and it was back in his arms again and his hand was ruffling its hair and it was climbing up over his shoulder and was diving over his back and his face was caressed by struggling body and thigh and it was standing on its hands, walking away on its hands and laughing.

'Aren't mornings wonderful?'

It was living what all those others had died to, had left behind, the sparkle of dew, the taste of the air, the breeze on one's face and the ancient awe of the rising sun. (Sun? was there a sun here?) He watched the creature laughing at him, jigging up and down on the wooden decking. This indeed was its own world.

'It's going to change,' it was telling him gleefully. 'Look what the breeze is bringing.' It was waving its hands at the scene, at the lake and standing trees and the retreating archways and then it stood stock-still, it was motionless with one hand pointing out in front of it.

As Nicholas turned he felt the touch of an intoxicating breeze, a return of the previous day's alarming enchantment swell over him. Where the creature was pointing the gold was changing to white, there was white blossom whirling and falling between the trees and now towards them across the lake, redolent with frightening spices, a storm of blossom. The place was a winter, the jade trees laden with white stretching away from the petal-covered lakeside in all directions. In the drunken air Nicholas could see the deer moving again, a line of tracks being left behind them, figures on a tinselled cake for a giant Christmas. Distant children were running over a powdered land. What had been golden was becoming a muted silver. The great bat came returning, floating, majestic and gliding, an airborne ghost, furry and benign, high over their heads.

Grabbed by the hand the monk found himself being propelled back into the house again. It was running, shouting, there was blossom in its hair, on its legs and body, over his habit. It was brushing against him, warm and dancing.

The house too had changed a little since Nicholas had got up. He did not remember the huge fireplace and now logs were burning and flames were flickering higher and higher and there was a glorious greeting from the scent of toast and hot coffee.

'Come on – get up everybody. A new morning —' it called. It capered round and round the hall, its voice echoing and re-echoing from the domes above them, a small bedlam.

Berenice got up slowly, wondering what she would wear, remembering that she had nothing and finding a wild silk blouse waiting, with a deeply orange summer skirt and sandals to match, and even a new set of familiar Marks and Spencer underwear, everything fitting. It was only after she had put it on that the rightness of the choice in fact impressed her. She found a pocket in the skirt with a clean handkerchief. It was some time – a time of dressing and hair brushing – before she was able to cope with the view through the window. And then again – it was difficult to be disoriented while eating an honest English breakfast.

'What are we supposed to do?' Berenice heard Oona inquire.

'Have some more coffee,' it said.

'We have a whole world,' Nicholas suggested.

And here we are, Berenice realized to herself. We are sitting about this comfortable fire looking at the hot yellow butter dripping through the good toast, here and now and at this moment. The taste is real, is particularly familiar. The mouth eats. Mycroft Charrington sprawls, chewing with relish and watching his wife and myself and Nicholas and this creature with a kind of excited intelligence interested in the next moment. Yesterday is slipping away. The days before even more so. We sit, we experience, we accept. It does not take long.

Usually she had breakfast at her window, looking down the Gloucester Road. In the evening with the lamplight the Italian Restaurant on the corner shines like a Christmas toy – that was one scene. But in the mornings the eye watches the approach of the postman (a letter from Mummy?) or catches the square and upright, rather disapproving electric milk-float that advances in jerks. There is that woman in the green coat who always leaves her door at ten past eight with a Pomeranian dog. Every morning one sees the old man who sweeps the street. One sees him sweeping round the parked cars and one must drag oneself from the window to wash one's plates and one's cup. You pick up your pencil and place its point on the paper. Every morning, to begin, that is the big decision. Every day you look at your own work hanging along the wall of the room, they are canvases, they are pieces of hardboard, each wearing a maze of tapestry colour, shapes without immediate meaning, two tiny figures running, far, minute, down in one corner, stretches of water or reflection or light or nothing. And this morning they would not have delivered the milk because the cows were no longer alive. There would be neither leaves nor Pomeranian dog. Yet she was drinking good coffee here and now and this morning.

It had eaten with them this time, happily, carelessly, crouching like an animal by the fireside, dropping butter on its skin, a primitive thing. It finished last, having eaten well. It wiped its hands on its thighs.

'I'll show you all the rest of the house.'

'There is no more of the house,' Mycroft said gently. 'We looked last night.'

'It wasn't snowing blossoms last night either,' it replied with an equal gentleness.

It laughed.

'Come on. Follow me.'

It began to jig again. They followed.

They were led outside first. The blossomfall had ceased and there was only a perfect carpeting of flowers on the wooden deck.

It led them down the metallic stairway towards the landing-stage and now they found that the punt was no longer there. They were right under the curving crystal side of the house, the translucent greys and the greens and at the other end of the floating stage there was a small door. The blossom was undisturbed. It had some difficulty dragging open the door. Mycroft helped it, scraping away the petals with his foot. The door was opened.

'Come inside.'

There was an illuminated vestibule with a door on either side. There were chairs, a long low table, a sense of chairs unsat on, a sense of waiting to go in. The creature opened the door on the left-hand side.

'You must all come into the studio.'

The studio was long with a great window opening almost on the level of the lake. In the distance they could see the now white shore through the trees that rose like pillars directly from the water and arched high back into the golden leaves above. In the water a black-skinned boy was wading, a froth of blossoms floating round his belly, a red cat upon his shoulder.

But it was the studio they saw. In the centre of the room there was a very tall easel mounted with a wide and primed but empty canvas. By its side, on a plain table, there were brushes, there were twelve bright and inviting tubes of paint lying in a perfect row and waiting to be squeezed. There was an empty palette. Then Oona's eye was attracted away, towards the right-hand wall. Here there were a row of finished pictures, mazes of tapestry colour, shapes without apparent meaning, stretches of water, of reflection, of light without perspective and no time.

Oona heard Berenice ask: 'But how did you bring them here? They were at the flat. That one was with my mother.'

The creature just stood there. It was chewing its nails.

'It was with your mother.'

'But the colours are all the right ones,' Berenice was saying, almost to herself.

'This is to be your studio,' it explained. 'You are staying here this morning. Every morning. Every day. This is yours. The others, they exist perhaps to see what you have done.'

Oona observed that Berenice was not listening to it, that she was looking eagerly along the line of finished pictures and then she came back and picked up one of the brushes and then she put the brush down.

'But how did you know that these were what I needed?'

It said nothing. It too was walking round the pictures, it was standing on the tips of its toes to look.

There was only one chair here and Berenice just sat down in it.

'That *is* yours,' it said, looking over a shoulder.

It was evident to Oona that Berenice had been given a whole self-contained world, that she was carried away, that she was not concerned with the rest of them. Berenice had got up from that chair and she walked down to the great window. She looked out transfixed, looked out at the lake under the arches, at the distant golden landscape. They only saw the blonde girl, the mass of hair falling to her waist, saw her hands reach out. There were pencils, empty sketch-books on a shelf. She was lost.

The portfolio that she had brought with her, her portfolio that she had had with her in the lift, in the punt, that was there too. She was distracted by the portfolio, it was a familiar friend, it had to be opened. Suddenly Berenice was like a child returning to a new toy in the morning.

The creature crouched beside her, enjoying her movement, looking at what she was looking at.

'Ahh!' it said.

Nicholas could see a sheet of paper on which had been drawn a crowd of milling people, people milling faceless in a huge advertising city, people who were loved but as yet possessed no face. As he stared he realized that only the crowd itself had been granted a face, the crowd that hurried nowhere like a whirlpool about the vehicles that were carrying a crowd in no direction. Only in one place, on a traffic island, was there an individual man and not just a movement of lines and a suggestion of people. He stood there quite at ease, unhurried, totally unconcerned, with a small white bird that perched on his hand. He was asking it a question, a question written under the cartoon in Berenice's neat italic hand:

'Yes. I heard what you said. But what do you mean?'

Then as her hand turned the sheets he saw another cartoon, a huge bridge being thrown across a river with immense gusto, vast cranes, excavators, scaffolding, a magnificent city on the far side, with tall willowing buildings and cantilevered terraces. There was an enjoyment in these man-made structures.

In the foreground an elegant well-dressed man spoke to an engineer. The man was evidently intelligent, in command of himself, unaffected by the enormous activity before him, by the immense bridge reaching towards his garden.

Here the caption read:

'But I explained to you before. I do not want to go across to the other side.'

Berenice looked for a moment at the creature beside her, then smiled. Her pencil began to move over her sketch-book. The face went serious, intent, far away.

The marks it made on the paper seemed to indicate nothing at the moment. They were only themselves.

Nicholas strained to look.

The creature was suddenly up and again on its feet and was capering back towards the others.

Oona opened her mouth to speak but the creature was quick to interpose. It pointed along the walls so that the rest of them had to look.

They looked again. These finished works had no captions, few figures hardly, except for Berenice herself. These were a series of self-imposed perspectives with differing colours and spaces in particular relation. The colours were a world that was as strange to them as the equally curious view beyond the enormous picture window.

The creature would not let them comment.

'I have other things to show you,' it was insisting. It would not let them look closer, either at Berenice's work or at what Berenice was now doing. It was shepherding them out again.

Berenice did not notice, did not hear either it or them. She was drawing.

It was shepherding them back, into the vestibule, across the carpet, through the other door. This was opened most carefully. Mycroft calculated that this other room took all the rest of the space occupied by the hall above them. It was no higher than the studio but was narrower and cunningly in-sloping to give the illusion of a greater height. Here it was grey and still. Mycroft let the door shut quietly. He was the last in. The tang of incense reached his mouth. Berenice had not come.

Thoughtfully, patiently, Mycroft Charrington examined these other surroundings. There was no window to look out of. Light entered through high slits cut into the stone walls, and it entered in a chosen direction. Here everything was stark, a relation of shape and angle and space. They were in a chapel with a single stone altar, two tall red candles burning, a high stone cross. The wall behind the altar had a plain black cloth suspended, embroidered only in one corner with the emblem of twin fishes. There was a sense of mourning. On the right-hand side, set in a niche and quite small, there was a figure of the Virgin. She stood in her blue (a battered worn and ancient blue) looking bold, looking curiously provocative, a girl's body definite under her robe. Mary in a kilt they called her.

Brother Nicholas turned up towards it and then down again to the creature standing beside him, alert, female, itself naked, its face half turned away.

'Nothing of the Museum of Victoria and of Albert has survived except for this,' it was saying.

The brother nodded slowly.

'This has always survived,' he said.

Then it left him, it was away and up to the altar. It ran up the steps, and twin shadows from the tall candles wavered across the walls. In front of the altar there were a series of stone slabs. There was a ring set in the slab at one end. For an instant it stood before the altar and then it turned aside and went down on one knee. The creature took hold of the ring and pulled. The stone was lifting like a lid.

'Come here, Brother Nicholas.'

Outside again a bell was tolling. Mycroft and Oona stood side by side, holding each other's hands, knowing something already from the creature's voice. Nicholas walked slowly, walked forward and up to the altar steps.

The creature was down on one knee, staring into the tomb. Without looking away it stretched out one hand to the monk who took it, who reached for the creature's hand almost automatically, who looked downward too. They saw him squeeze the hand hard and they heard him give a small cry. He looked away.

'Look again, Nicholas,' the creature said. 'Look again

because you know him. He is your friend. You are not afraid to look at your friend.'

The bell tolled above their heads, louder, more slowly, seemingly nearer now. Nicholas looked down into the tomb, into the space that had been opened, his lips moved; his hand, slightly, on a minute scale, offered his blessing, his fingers reached down and touched the face out of view in the huge stone coffin.

'Father Prior,' they heard him say, 'may peace be with you.' They saw Nicholas look up then, look up at the creature standing before him. It was looking down, looking down at the familiar face with him. Mycroft had to strain to hear any words.

'There lies a man.'

Then for a moment the little monk could not speak. Then:

'Why didn't you rescue him, rather than myself?'

As they looked it was for a moment as if all expression, all person, was wiped off the creature's face. It was shaking its head. Its mouth began speaking.

'I could not bring them all,' it said. It was answering a different question. 'They were not all there to bring. I brought only your Prior. I brought him that you might know that you are not yet dead. Your new friends, they are not dead. Your deaths are still to come. They will be another problem, another question. But at the present you must learn not to ask any questions – not out loud. You can think – you can wait – you can endure. For the present, Brother Nicholas, you must remain to know yourself.'

It bent down and slowly replaced the slab. For an instant Nicholas tried to prevent this. The girl creature kissed him on the forehead but insisted. He turned away. It settled the stone back in place and came away from the altar.

The brother was on his knees.

The bell still tolled.

Mycroft Charrington noted the creature's walk back towards Oona and himself, realizing for the first time that their own turn had come, noting its fixed, now unconsidered expression as it walked towards them, unhurried, continuing. Its surroundings, the plain grey chapel with the steeply raked walls, the altar with its cold remains, these things did not affect it. Mycroft realized that they had affected himself, the wooden Virgin and the praying monk before the high black cross – not his world but a world within itself nevertheless – as the bright outward gazing studio had been a world.

It was pointing towards the door.

'Later you may want to come. You may want to come – you may want to understand these places. But now we will leave, for him, for yourselves. He must know this place alone.'

They looked and they found themselves realizing that this was so – that the presence of the dead man, the presence of Nicholas whom they knew, gave the place a particular reality – the shadows, the candlelight, they ceased to be a theatre and became an understanding.

It was speaking:

'What he wants, and not only wants but knows,

possesses and contemplates, it is everywhere. But here there is a reminder, a point of focus. We will leave him.'

They were back, out in the vestibule, walking on the soft carpet in a different place. They were led out, back through the doorway to the outside, the blossoming drifting away, the gold flowing and tingling through the tree-tops.

It led them up the metal stairway, up to the decking and the now familiar yellow creepers. They followed its feet.

Mycroft reached out for Oona, his narrow face considering hers, considering her carefully piled hair (he too could put it together – once when she had burnt her hands he had dressed it for her, carefully, elegantly and under her precise instruction). They followed the eager girl thing together. The blossoms were dispersing now, petals blowing and scurrying under its feet, falling into the water below them. It led them on like a small dog, across the wooden decking, back the way they had come and into the house.

Unexpectedly – it was quite unchanged. The fire perhaps had burned a little lower. The breakfast remained uncleared. The beds were still unmade. There was a vague air of crumbs and desolation.

'Sit down,' it said, pointing to the chairs by the pool. They found themselves walking over the blue-green tiles, automatically they found their own chairs, they were sitting down.

It fed the fish. It said nothing.

They waited.

Then it got up and went to a cupboard in the wall. Opened it, was a wardrobe with a full-length mirror inside the door. It began, very earnestly, to dress.

There was very fresh clean white underwear, a slight breath of lavender, briefs, white socks, a hardly necessary bra, a very thoughtful assessment in the mirror. It brushed the short black hair. It combed endlessly. Then it remembered its slip. It combed again. There were a pair of long white socks, a crisp white blouse, a cleaned and pressed immaculate blue kilt. There were usual ordinary girl's shoes. It fussed over itself. It washed its face. When at last it had quite finished it closed the wardrobe door.

'Excuse me,' it said. It was looking rather anxious. There was no capering.

'Do I look all right?'

'You want to pull your slip up behind,' Oona said.

It smiled and hitched.

It was a daughter.

'The others will be back at lunch-time,' it said shyly. 'There will be a lunch. If you don't mind I shall have to be away for a while. . . .'

It looked at them with childlike concern.

'You will be all right won't you? I mean here. You are the married ones you see. I must go.'

It was even picking up a small handbag from Nicholas's chair. For a moment it was almost indecisive. It was so neat – it smiled vaguely – it let itself out and was gone.

There was a pause.

'And all that too,' Mycroft said as his fingers explored

the brand-new shirt he was wearing, 'all that was un-doubtedly intended.' He stretched himself in the arm-chair.

Oona was looking about them. Not far from where they sat was a row of tall bookshelves in a pool of golden light.

'Darling,' she said quietly, 'they are all your books up there.'

They both stood up. They looked round them. There were a number of other things: Oona's African work-basket, an elegant jug from off their window-sill at home.

Yet somehow they did not want to look too closely. The coloured patterns of light from the transparent domes, the calculated shadows, these things still arched over their heads, unexpected, shaped and curiously foreign.

'I think we will begin by making all the beds,' Mycroft suggested.

There was no reply.

Mycroft looked round.

Oona was now standing beside her bed. It took Mycroft several moments to understand, so familiar was the framed photo in her hand, the photograph that was always beside her bed at home, the portrait of Geoffrey when he was ten, his cricket shirt unfastened at the neck.

But she was not looking at it. She only pointed to the equally familiar tattered box – *They* had not provided a new one – Geoffrey's beloved old meccano box, the bat-tered pieces projecting out of the sides.

Mycroft found himself shutting his eyes, shutting them tightly, not wanting to speak, not wanting even to think.

Oona speaking very softly:

'They are so bloody bloody cruel.'

And he must look at her and she was looking only desperately broodingly grim:

He was just listening to her voice:

'We must be thankful that we have been rescued and we must remember that we have a duty to other people, persons who are strangers. Of course I have seen a great many people die and of course I am used to it. Strange, unnatural to want, just wanted at least to have been allowed to see the death of our own dear son.'

Mycroft had stopped thinking because now Oona was important, more important.

'Do you remember the old days when Geoffrey wasn't? We were together. I always like to think we remember the time we started Geoffrey, that afternoon, you had just lost a case, you were so glad to come back to me. But Geoffrey has *been*. Geoffrey was worth while – always, always?'

'Always, Mycroft,' she said with her lips trembling.

He saw, by his own bedside, two stone wine cups. They had not been there before. They were full, a green and sparkling liquid that was not wine. He brought them over.

'After we have drunk this,' he said, 'we will try . . . We will try and make the beds.'

She nodded. She could only take the cup from him.

The drink was not a sedative, it was not a stimulant. There was only the sense of restoration, the almost immediate feeling of solidity, stolidity, a more positive existence.

'Mycroft —'

Pause.

'Mycroft.'

'Yes, Oona.'

'At least Nicholas had – saw – a body. We only have words and this place. This place isn't true, is it? It's not real like we are real – like Geoffrey is real. This place doesn't exist, does it?'

'I don't know, my dear. I only know that I exist. I can only believe that you are here.'

She put out a hand for him and their fingers clasped. The blissful certainty of actual touch.

They kept on seeing more of their own things, a vase, her sewing-machine, a paper knife.

Calm was forcing itself upon them.

10

Berenice was particularly, absolutely and splendidly alone.

To paint – suddenly to be free of suffocating demanding contemporary – no not criticism – fashion. To be free of that faint, continuing and wondering sense of inferiority.

To pace the sheer extent of this studio, hers, hers with the materials – here there was no restriction.

Mother would not come here.

The odd respect one had for Mummy – the sudden seeing of Mummy as a whole life now. (It was a whole life now, Berenice.) The confession to oneself – the fact that one had always known – that here finally and always one had wanted to be without Mummy's experience, her experience of Mummy. One had to face that odd and always present desire of wanting Mother to be dead. All the time the fear, the realization, that one's habits, one's taste, one's judgements were a shadow triumphant of kindly Mummy in her big solitary and immaculate house.

Sit here and let one's pencil feel on the paper, feel the shape of those greening archways.

Now she could remember quite calmly her own especial

discovery – that discovery about Bruce. Bruce had not merely become her own revolt against Mummy. To be adult was to know familiarly his male company, to contact his particular slanting vision, his drawing of her torso over and over again, his objects were always drained of their person. Bruce's hunger for herself, her praise, her imitation, her services. To feel him within her, to be an animal under him, to be what he wanted. To suddenly meet in Bruce's mocking sensuality, Mummy all over again.

She stood firm here in this studio.

Here there was nobody's hunger to feed.

The studio was benign – to draw a shape that was entirely her own conception – now. Here was a shape for the others to see and enjoy for its very own sake. They were not to come and look because lovely Berenice had drawn it.

She stabbed at the paper with the pencil for neither Mummy nor Bruce would ever see what she could do now – dearest Mummy with her endless arrangements of flowers in the big bay window – Bruce demanding that his girl should scrub his back in the bath: the shattered bay window, the bath water vanished in sudden scalding steam, the bath folded like a molten rat trap.

Bruce never liked tears.

Mummy always said that her little girl never cried.

They enjoyed doing ordinary things.

They found everything very easily, dusters, a broom, even a vacuum cleaner. The regular routine of chores enabled them to follow a pattern. There was no flex to the vacuum cleaner – but then Mycroft remembered that there had been no electric light either – only illumination. He switched the cleaner on and it made no sound – it only worked. He did not investigate this there and then, he was merely amused by it. There would be time enough. They were not going anywhere. There was nowhere to go to.

He found Oona's knitting-machine, the machine she had bought in a fit of enthusiasm and then had never had time to master and had lost the instructions. There was a new set of instructions tucked into the middle of the works. There was a good supply of the correct ply wool in a pale maroon that Oona rather liked.

On the bottom shelf, under the books, Mycroft found a sequence of files covering a project that he had worked on some three years ago, a project right outside his normal scope. It was a scientific project as the subject for a film. It was to be a careful, deliberate and measured account of an experiment. But this was not to be an experiment with different coloured mice in cages. It was to be an account of an experiment with human beings. Half a million identical human twins were to be set apart from one another in two identical luxury camps. The camps would have no contact with each other and no contact with the rest of the world. They would have precisely equal resources. Of the two Camp 'A' would be endowed with a capitalist way of life and Camp 'B' with a communist régime. The camps were to be sealed off for twenty years and then examined.

For the first time there was to be a proper objective

experiment. There was to be no nonsense about what people thought they wanted, there was to be a systematic trial and experiment. For the first time in politics they would really try to find out.

Mycroft's result, when the camps were at last opened for examination, was quite simple. The capitalist camp had rebelled against free enterprise and had become communist. The communist camp had thrown off its rigid centralized system and had become capitalist. Both camps were living very well.

As so often the experiment answers the question that nobody had thought to ask.

Mycroft enjoyed re-reading his notes and files.

No coffee arrived at eleven o'clock but they did find their own coffee service and a replica of their old (very old) Cona coffee machine, milk, coffee, an electric ring. Well it was not wired to anything but it seemed to be electric. There was a switch. It became hot.

There were no bells ringing outside – only silence. Up to now, they did not understand why, there had been no real inducement to look out of the windows. Outside was not real. They did not want the outside to be real.

They sat drinking coffee. There was no need for conversation very much. They sat still.

Mycroft gazed down at the pool with the two fishes. Oona stretched out her legs and felt the whole of herself seated in her chair.

'Have you noticed,' she said out of the blue, 'that we have not asked it any real questions? We have hardly asked ourselves any real questions since we have been down here. I feel, in the middle of so much strangeness, so much that is unusual, impossible; I feel drained of curiosity. I don't want to know anything just at the moment. I just sit.'

Mycroft's fingers walked over his knees. His eyes narrowed following their independent locomotion with a kind of distant interest.

'I know what you mean,' he said. 'We are having a rest from questions. Sometimes one has to stop asking questions, pursuing thoughts. It is more important to wait. I feel that there is a question but at the moment I am refusing to consider it. Probably we will receive the answer even before we have so much as framed it. I suspect that we shall do just precisely and exactly as the conductor of this experiment intends.'

Mycroft was cleaning an old horse-brass. They had found it in a junk shop in Kensington about a fortnight ago for a few shillings. They had been meaning to clean it. He had just found it again in one of the cupboards beside a rag and a tin of Brasso, silently accusing him.

There was a long pause. Mycroft was busy, his long fingers curled round the edge of the brass. He was cleaning.

Nobody came up. No actual person appeared. There were no disturbances.

No disturbances – boyhood in a Pembrokeshire summer, the insects hovering over thistles on the field above the sea. Charles Morning sitting in the grass beside him, saying little, lobbing him an apple, a sail on a little boat fluttering, the boat's bows hesitating, tacking. 'There she goes,' Charles Morning said. There was no urgency, there was never any particular hurry with Charles. They had a secret beach from which they would bathe when the tide was low. You had to go down sheer cliffs to it. 'Shall we swim?' Charles said. 'Only swim if you want to.' Sometimes he just watched Charles – Charles had no urgency, one was at peace, one pleased oneself – he was like a seal in the water. The smell of Charles beside him in the sunshine, the tang of the salt on his skin, the insects above the thistles, just sitting on the rock and casting stones into the sea.

Oona was casting the wool on her knitting-machine, comfortably and without hurry and was following the instructions.

Once she said: 'I think this is what it means.' It was not really addressed to her husband, it was addressed to the air.

Lunch was in no way her concern. She had only to be here.

'I suppose,' Mycroft was saying, 'that the main disadvantage in being taken away from one's research programme is that one no longer has any excuse to avoid thinking about the data that one has already assembled.'

Oona gave one of her old familiar grins.

'As a doctor,' she began in her best consulting-room tone, 'I propose to spend my time writing a challenging thesis on the problem of being well.'

'On reflection I think we have to remember that it is we who are the objects of research now.'

The knitting-machine began to perambulate around its rows.

'Perhaps we always were,' she said.

He observed that a door was open. He had no memory of that door being there before. This did not matter. He caught Oona's eye. They got up together and investigated it.

There was a kitchen.

There were four plates warming on the stove, serving spoons waiting. A note on grey paper:

MOUSAKA IN THE OVEN.

The oven was on, there was mousaka there, almost done.

The stove was one model more up-to-date than Oona's own, but not so up-to-date that she did not understand it. The cupboard over the working space opened silently to the touch. It was some moments before Oona realized what it was that made the interior so familiar. The groceries were not merely her accustomed brands, they were in an identical position (illogical as this sometimes was) to her own cupboard at home. There were two differences. The packets were unopened and where possible they were a larger size.

At one end of the working surface there was a large bowl of stewed dried fruit, four little bowls, a jug of cream.

Oona looked round carefully.

'We are being weaned back to a kind of normality,' she said thoughtfully. 'This time we must take some food out of an oven, serve it on to plates, carry it to the table. To that extent we must serve our own meal. It is oddly thought out – they have made this our kitchen and yet not our kitchen. Everything is in the same relative place but it is a little better, or a little bigger. I would say that this room is about a foot wider than the kitchen at home.'

'Which we have always said we would have liked. If the theory is correct we will find on the bottom shelf of that other wall cupboard, by the sink unit, my pipe and presumably a new tin of Gold Block tobacco.'

He walked over to it, opened it, and laughed.

'A new pipe. Three tins of Gold Block.'

Oona had been examining the mousaka. It was a favourite dish. There was a new oven-cloth to hand. She looked at her watch and closed the oven door.

'I would say five minutes,' she said. 'And I would say that at the appropriate moment the others will appear.'

She put the oven-cloth down.

'You know, Mycroft, I have a different diagnosis of this situation. I don't think that this is a matter of research by Them. I think that they know far too much about us already. I think this is more like an education of us.'

Mycroft nodded. His long fingers were exploring his face, his eyes were looking round him everywhere.

'To teach the mice to explore the maze.'

'No – not that perhaps. It is the fact that we are – as we are – that interests them. Not how we are, not why. It may be the *experience that we are* that They are looking at.'

Mycroft looked at her approvingly; his mind working up and down over a new structure of possibility.

'Perhaps,' he suggested, 'they watch, not us but our unique view outwards, out into the world and out into ourselves, each of us bounded by our own intricate and elegantly adjusted ignorance. (How do I know that what I see as blue you do not see as green? We only know that we give each other consistent answers.) Perhaps our pairs of eyes are just a different scanning camera through which they see from their eternal omnipresent vantage point the world split into time and space.'

They looked at each other. They both knew that for the moment neither would say anything further. It was sufficient to ponder.

Mycroft Charrington felt himself to be flooded with the pleasure of being himself, of simply standing here in this kitchen with Oona.

'We can be certain of nothing,' he said.

He had noticed that there was a white venetian blind over the window. One could not easily look out. He did not try. At the moment he did not want to. It was enough to be in here, to consider these problems.

Oona was standing beside him, with her back to the white tiles of the kitchen wall. She was looking over her shoulder through the open door into the hall. Quickly she looked away.

'There is something there,' she said. 'No, not the others. Something is laying the table, I think. No, not it, something else. I don't want to see at the moment. Close the door for me.'

He closed the door, slowly, carefully, and without looking. They could not now be tempted to look. It would be like asking a question. They did not want to ask direct questions. Oona smiled at him.

They were not alarmed now. Only patient.

Mycroft raised his hand and touched her face and she leaned slightly against him, her feet a little apart from one another, and they stood there listening to each other's breathing.

'A new home,' he said. 'Though for some reason we seem to be sharing it with two others. They are an interesting problem.'

'Not a problem,' he heard her say. 'A mystery. But I feel certain that They have thought of all this. Their reasons will come to light in due course. I suppose that we have to realize that one just has to accept mystery. One must remember to accept that one does not know.'

They stood quite still. Oona could feel the touch of his familiar fingers. They were together.

'Mycroft. Oona.' It was the voice of Brother Nicholas. They smiled. They had begun to like him.

It was an unexpectedly pleasant afternoon. Brother Nicholas had insisted on washing-up that luncheon, and Oona had insisted on helping him. Mycroft had been trying to explain to Berenice, not what he was trying to discover with his experiments but why he should be trying at all – not for the end result – 'Yes,' they heard him say, 'I agree, the end result, the good of mankind, better health, etc. etc., but NO. NO. NO. THAT is not

124

why I go to a laboratory every day. THAT is not the fascination that made me study, that makes me search now . . .'

The monk, Oona was amused to find, was nothing if not capable about a kitchen, familiar with plastic bowls and detergent and methodical stacking; talking to her knowledgeably about cooking. A half smile played on the monk's face.

Oona found herself moving from the subject of fresh trout to her new sense of an undisturbed peace. No telephone could ring, no child could sicken, no emergency occur. There was the golden lake and the fathomless light and no possible communication and they put the plates away together – there was a rack. Oona did not have to think where things went, here were the same places where she had always put things, and she was describing children's diseases to him, the special problems of the young growing body (and he was interested), the odd difference in actually dealing with her own son, the hospital in Holborn where she was known by so many people, the faces of children dying, potentials without a future, and now there was no hospital, no children – and she described a wonderful method of cooking spinach with butter and how one should re-cook it on five successive days (Gluttony? – 'No, art,' Nicholas said) and Nicholas was again amused by her.

'We are marooned,' he said, 'like a lifeboat in a calm at sea. It is a very comfortable lifeboat. But the world too was for us, in England, a very comfortable lifeboat, but we were on a lifeboat just the same.'

The monk also talked about his monastery, trying to give very simply to Oona the reasons why he happened to believe in God (and had they such extra reasons to disbelieve just now?), and why he should want to express his belief in the way he did, in that Community, with its regular movement of labour and sacrament, ritual and patient forethought through the year.

(The dish-mop thrusting over the casserole dish.)

'No, we do not dislike women, nor do we hate the body, there is no truth in this at all – these are irrelevant conceptions. It is rather that we have contacted; not always as often, nor as clearly, nor as closely as we would wish; something more powerful still. One falls in love, as it were, in another direction.'

(And it is whispered that if a man should marry a woman whom he loves, and she him, and if he is faithful to her; yet how does he know that his neighbour's daughter would not please him more? Or an even greater joy, that he might exquisitely please her? Perhaps she has some treasure that his own beloved wife does not possess. Perhaps he can pluck in her some harpstring of joy which no other man could play. But of course only God can be, know, express, experience: everything. Each man must have that faith and patience to stick to his own last, to be only himself, to remember that his failures too, are favours. We must content ourselves with one life at a time in our own eternity. We must accept the tragedy implicit in each of our own limitations.)

He remembered his cousin Astrid kissing him feverishly when her sister Margaret was not looking. He had liked

Astrid more than he had understood, but she had bewildered him. He remembered seeing Margaret running in the distance towards the sea, a long way away over the sands, and the smell of the sun on Astrid's flesh. She had wanted him to touch her hair, her legs, had wanted him to see her and he had felt bewildered at himself. He had also been bewildered that first day, the day he had entered the monastery, putting down his small suitcase – the smell of polished floors – and now there would be no pride, only obedience and love, to clean, to labour and to wait. The pain in his back after the polishing, the voices of men at prayer. Like the dear voices of the Abbey church, Astrid had been a dear face, a true favour, each to the time, each to the place.

They went out and found Mycroft sitting and Berenice drawing him, her eye moving over the watching face, looking back at him as he lay on the bed. They were talking, spasmodic remarks, rushes of conversation that drifted away to silences, her pen moving continually over the paper.

'You see,' Berenice had explained, 'it is like looking out of a window – one must want to look out of a window. . . .'

'To understand? To understand what?'

The pen paused on the paper.

'To hold a world still while one sees: people, things, persons, objects – and then to see them in a separate way, as shapes, tones, textures and voices. Even if they are moving – of course everything is moving – but even that movement itself must in a way be held and known. One must feel *now,* so that others can re-feel with me, can make another and new *now,* the experience. This is being alive.'

Her pen moved on again, quickly making shapes on the paper.

Mycroft did not try to see the actual drawing. It was some time before her words began again. He sat there, observing the brown face speaking.

'You see, I try to see the pattern – as yet the pattern is not real at your level, any more than your feelings are real at mine. This pattern, my pattern, when I have discerned it, is a way of holding the moving motionless, of seeing something in such a way that it corresponds with what is in myself. Then I must try to throw to you: a bridge.'

He sat there comfortably while Berenice talked to him, seeing in his own mind the ordered flow in his own laboratory – of cultures forming in tubes, of the myriad battalions of mice feeding, of the analysis of the perpetual flow of often irrelevant statistics. He sat watching as his wife, as Brother Nicholas entered the room, his wife's tall mass of carefully piled hair, the quiet smile of the little monk with her. He was so comfortable that the outside reality of the calm jade forest trees, the soft blossoms and the sylvan glades seemed to be sliding away from under his fingers.

A new pattern, his own pattern, had already developed in his mind, a protective pattern, a reply for the time being, an answer until new facts and new theories came to put it down. He would not look up, he did not look outside. Firmly he kept his mind within the house. Ideas began to move like a constant beam through a prism, a beam that became divided, meaningful. He began to project on to his mind a series of coloured diagrams, a three-dimensional model erected in merging spirals, an effort to simplify the complex.

But the chair was soft under his body, the green tiles under his feet led in modulated tones to the edge of the quiet pool, the twin fish hovering and at peace. There was the row of beds, with their plain grey rugs, the curved and coloured domes above them with their fantastic lights. The bells began to peal joyfully again, willy-nilly penetrating his mind. Truth was being overtaken by reality.

II

From memory it had not really taken them very long to reach the lake from the lifts. They were all agreed on that. They had not really thought about it very much before.

If you looked out of the windows of the house the whole place – the whole country – seemed to stretch into an indefinite distance.

A cave? An illusion? A translation through space time? Or instead of asking questions – the single concept of sitting still, of not looking, of remaining, of not going outside.

It took them nearly an hour of discussion (not discussion Oona thought afterwards – just talking) before it actually occurred to them to venture out together. Not to go anywhere – not to have any particular plan. One place was as good as another.

'Just to go for a walk,' Berenice said. 'One has to get the feel of a place just to know that one has arrived.'

'We shall not go anywhere with a definite intention,' Mycroft stated, careful to define their intentions. 'I do not think that we ought to say to ourselves that we are trying to find anything.'

'It is often good,' Brother Nicholas reminded them at one point, 'to observe without comment, without judgement, but to see and to wait without hurry, without impatience, all things in their own time.'

It was not odd, Mycroft decided, that they should find walking shoes, that they should find shorts, a grey-green shirt, a slightly eccentric walking-stick with knobbles. Oona and Berenice were changing into cool and white classic frocks. Only Brother Nicholas was excused from dressing up.

'We are not even certain that the emergency has actually occurred,' Berenice had been saying. 'We have only been told.'

'There is the body of my friend and superior,' Nicholas had reminded them.

'We do not know the truth,' Mycroft said.

But it was Nicholas who repeated to them: 'We are just going out for a long walk. We are going to deny ourselves both intentions and judgements.'

They did not look back at the house when they left it. They would return later. It had been comfortable. Somehow they found it more of an effort to walk out of this building under their own power than they had expected. Yet they were making the effort. They opened the door. They went out.

It seemed that they had almost forgotten the golden world outside. It poured in on them from all directions, a kind of yearning, an impelling, an atmosphere that bubbled through their emotions.

Somehow they had expected the punt to be missing

from the landing-stage. They had supposed vaguely, without admitting it aloud, that they were prisoners in the house. But there the punt was waiting, tied up again in its place. They all climbed down the metallic stairway. There was no sound, no wind. There was nobody about.

Here they were, all standing in a row along the floating landing-stage, Mycroft clasping his walking-stick, almost uncertain as to what he should do with it. Berenice held the punt. They climbed in. Nicholas took charge of the pole.

There were no difficulties. They cast off. They pushed out into the stream.

In the first moments of this actual start they had left the house without actually looking round them. Now, seated at ease in the punt they again found themselves floating in a cathedral of golden light, the still water reflecting the rising jade-like pillars that reached up to archway after archway, through aisle after aisle, reaching up into their bronze illuminated leaf-smothered ceiling. Everywhere the light seemed to be in faintly trembling motion while they themselves moved across the mirror of lake water, the monk their patient ferryman. A flotilla of ducks passed them by, mandarin, resplendent and royal. There were harbours and islands and continents of lilies, purples and oranges, rafts of leaves in black and ancient silver. In the distance plants flamed up along the lake shore, in one place rising like a high fountain, scarlets and purples cascading, the leaves and branches invisible behind them.

Again Nicholas felt himself to be seized by a whiff of

intoxicating exuberance. Lyrically he was pushing at a pole, a wand, a magic staff.

Oona's hand gripped tight on his sandalled foot. Now she was pointing, out towards their left, out through the tunnel of archways and in that direction the distant shore rose in a huge terraced staircase of copper-coloured fields upward and upward and nearest to them Nicholas could see a party of white unicorn grazing on edelweiss, their spiral horns tipped and shining.

'Look,' Oona was now saying and pointing and there were a pair of vast bats gliding through the archways, graceful and swaying, caparisoned like palfreys without riders, turning now, banking away from them, incredible and beautiful. Suddenly they commenced flapping and there was the eerie side to side bat movement, the alarming acceleration, they were climbing upward and vertical and gone from them.

Nicholas returned to his familiar physical action, the poling of the punt.

'I have seen them before,' he was confessing, but Oona was not listening to him.

'A whole zoology – a whole new world of life here.'

Mycroft was nodding at her, smiling and staring. (Like the clothes, like the house, this place has everything. It fascinates us, Oona and me. Creatures like harlequins, bats out of paradise, perhaps even bacteria lovely as a dragonfly. But what is this show being put on *for*? There were no answers.)

Now they were coming in towards the shore and at moments it was almost as if the punt itself was motionless, as if it was the shore that was moving towards them, that it was the tall columns that were stalking by.

'There are children over there,' Mycroft began.

They were boys with streaming hair, swimming under them like a school of fishes, speeding under their bows with long feet quivering, rainbow bubbles running from their mouths.

Oona stared down at them intently. She had taught Geoffrey to swim, it was a long time before he could swim as fast as Oona Charrington, and Geoffrey had learned well. She had taught crippled children to swim, swimming with them herself and being with them through the excitement of learning a first freedom from their own twisted bodies.

'They are not children,' she murmured, 'they are only made to look like children, they are not even human, we cannot breathe in that way for so long.'

'They are not children,' Mycroft echoed sadly.

Berenice was in a silence of looking, her mouth tasting, limbs swimming.

The boys had taken no notice of the punt, no notice of their watching, they were vanishing up-lake.

Nicholas poled the punt onwards. When Mycroft signalled he would change direction. In the distance the unicorn were moving, galloping and away between the tree trunks. He poled them on.

Fruit, plump and glistening, floated on the water, maroon and yellow. Berenice plucked some and tasted.

. . . a sharp, acute, aware taste.

'We will go ashore here,' Mycroft said. The richness

of the lake, the enclosing clutching realness disturbed him.

Brother Nicholas swung them, easily, a practised well-judged movement of the pole, the sandalled feet gaining purchase on the decking. Berenice was in the water up to her knees, laughing, pulling them in. Oona hung over the edge of the punt, for she had seen new fishes, fishes transparent and darting, their complex guts like coloured jewels. Her fingers reached out towards them in the water and they switched away.

Nicholas laid down the pole with care, remembering the last time Astrid had visited him at Cambridge, the sunshine of that gloriously soft and splendid, gentle and horrible afternoon. Mycroft looked ahead. He landed first. The ground was rising. In this direction the trees, the columns, seemed closer together. He helped Oona out, Nicholas out. They all pulled the punt ashore.

Oona drifted towards some pale anaemic-looking flowers.

'How do you think these reproduce?' she was asking.

Mycroft led them straight inland. Nicholas and Berenice found themselves together, walking behind in step, suddenly enjoying an earlier familiarity. Nicholas touched Berenice's hand and was not certain that it was by accident.

'See the cat.' Mycroft was pointing with his stick to the far side of the clearing, his other hand reaching out to Oona's shoulder.

'It's got a ruff, a black and white ruff. Look at the tail kink – a kind of giant siamese with long fur.'

And then they saw it stop short, a flashed intelligent stare in their direction, a kind of sideways dance, and then up, up the jade trunk, like lightning with a kind of 'WRoow'.

Here they were walking, it did not matter where to, there was no particular direction, they were walking into the forest, under the trees, the golden archways alive with flowers.

Now, Berenice was the first to see, it was more sombre, roses in deepest purple, the gold dulled by great age, the grass merging itself into a field of black. A different *tone*.

'Like the church in Holy week,' she said, quite brilliantly to Nicholas. 'When everything is in a shroud.'

They were deliberately holding hands.

Nicholas smiled. He was accepting that he now lived in an impossible place filled with unexpected moments, the endless stimulation of novelty, the experience of extreme and gratuitous comfort that he had not earned. He was conscious, as his feet walked here, of an immense well-being, of Astrid's fingers, of the fingers of Berenice, of my dear Lady whom my Lord hath given, now and for ever.

That morning, kneeling in the chapel (the chapel under the house that reflected so perfectly the taste and style of his Order, in simplicity and chastity, the stark grandeur of his religion, the gentleness of living hands), his mouth repeated the familiar words of his daily office. Not the Office for the Dead. Father Prior would not have asked for that now, not at that moment. There were so many dead. They were another concern and at a different place.

'It is very grave – just here,' Nicholas agreed.

(And yet – 'For thou Lord has made me glad through thy work: I will triumph in the works of thy hands.') (The pleasure of Berenice walking over the black grass, her brown feet seeming pale now.)

That morning he had been alone with the Prior and had remembered him. 'Of what use, my son, is a tune if you cannot remember the previous notes, or a symphony, if you cannot recall the earlier themes, or a story, if at the end you have forgotten the beginning?' The still face had laughed at him, with him, in kindness. Now the Prior was no longer. Now there was only Nicholas, conscious that he too wore the mantle of his Order and conscious that this was sufficient for him. To remain here within this place, that was enough. If he was to leave, if he was to go elsewhere, that was enough also.

They both walked over the black grass in silence, listening to Oona talking about the scarlet beetles running at their feet.

On the right hand of the chapel (the only chapel now), Nicholas remembered the figure of the Virgin brought down from the Kensington Museum, still the survivor, still waiting, still facing the world with her absolute certainty of mercy. She was only a small enigmatic wooden figure, carved in love, carved perhaps in awe of what was made. It dared and reminded, it lasted, it endured. Mary in her kilt was always.

'Chastity,' the Prior had once said to him, the wind

whipping Novemberwise over the deserted beach where they were walking, 'Chastity does not consist of refusing to reproduce. Nor does chastity consist of reproducing out of duty. (There are many people in the world. God is in no hurry. He holds eternity in his hands. Man is summoned to life's banquet, not to a stale bite at a quick-lunch counter.) Chastity consists of an unselfish love in the full joy of one's partner – we have been married, Nicholas, we know that that alone is no simple thing – and before the presence and in the knowledge of our God. So often the faithful forget that God disdains neither the parings of our toenails nor the immortality of our souls.'

They had wandered under another archway. Here in this next clearing the leaves themselves were black above their heads and they were cast in shadow. Beyond them it was light again.

A biological reason? – Mycroft was asking himself. Then he stopped still.

'Oona. What is that?'

It was Berenice who first realized what it was. At this distance one could not see it clearly, but for the moment she was content to contemplate it at this distance, to accept what it told her here. There would be time enough to go nearer, to see it in other ways.

It was a carved rock.

They saw a rock coming straight out of the black grass, coming both upwards and outwards from the surface of the ground, an outward explosion of static stone thighs, belly, whole torso of a wide squat woman, torso with head, the whole with a twisted outflung furious tension yet with a going, the straddling thighs and great domed belly giving birth downward and inward and back into the earth.

They went forward and looked up at it in silence. They found that none of them were making any comment. What was rock was also labouring flesh and what had been caught alive was in motionless rock. There was a face. It was not that it was unbeautiful but that it might be dangerous to see. They looked away.

'Why,' Mycroft wondered, 'are we exposed to this? Why are we allowed to find this sort of object? Why don't they realize (who is to realize?) that we do not want any more experience, that we have seen enough, that there has been too much to see when all we want to do is to sit still and hold our heads and catch our breath? Are we to be converted to – converted to what? Are we being brain-washed or brain-drowned into just being in this world? Am I going to be made to forget everything that I ever was or ever did? (Perhaps that would be the best thing – the only thing.) But the house was a kind of reminder of what we were. Yet what do I want to do? Publish a bloody learned paper to be lost with a million other papers in an unthumbed collection of scientific abstracts? But I only want to play with a coloured ball with Geoffrey on the beach – beach trays and the taste of sand in the tea. But instead they make us live on a diet of port and peaches when all we ask for is blessed dry bread!'

Nicholas considered the figure, knowing that it tried to

express an emotion, a knowledge beyond what he would have considered discreet, what for most men would be wise. Yet it existed. One did not look away. One waited, remembering to be oneself.

Berenice wanted to stand almost underneath it, to put a hand out and touch its contours, to put her face within inches of the carved rock, to ask no questions about it, but to go off in another direction and look at it again. She had let go of the monk's hand. He was standing quite still. She was running everywhere.

Birth was something that Oona was familiar with – an obvious symbol – to her a cool technical problem. But for that reason both more compelling as well as less perhaps. She was made to think back to that girl in the self-service store in labour under the corn flakes on a newspaper – without the usual clinical trimmings, without any preparation so that the connection with what she was doing and ordinary daily life had been closer. Her handbag still lying within a few feet of her, her wire basket of groceries carefully set down, the shapeless flowered dress just pulled back from her open thighs and that still extraordinary moment of the baby's head coming out on to the world, to support it in the palm of one's hand. That Saturday Oona had had her shopping free.

It caught her eye, a little bundle of white wool on hooves skipping and dodging across the shadows of the forest, coming back to them to gallop away from them, it uttered hoarse little laughs. It shied away from her hand, and then came nearer.

'There's a blue one,' Berenice said, and there were several, they were waltzing and twirling, pirouetting and fluffy with a clattering of tiny hooves.

Everybody was being distracted from the stone figure.

Oona was very patient. After several starts and alarms the white one let her tickle the woolly neck and it licked her fingers with a little tongue. She sat on the black grass and in a moment or two she was surrounded by a small herd of them, miniature lamas in white and black and brown and powder blue, crowding and bleating, bouncing vertically up and down on their feet, all excited at her company, little stringy tails waggling, and some-how gay and excited with each other's presence, jostling and demanding, bright yellow eyes alight with . . . amusement.

'But it is amusement,' Oona said out loud, for when she laughed they responded, their faces flickered with com-plex expressions, for they had not only general amuse-ment but amusement between themselves. It was as if they talked to each other with expressions, the attention of the eye, the angle of the ear, the movement of the whole fleecy body.

'Do you see the youngsters?' Mycroft was pointing.

The little ones were on the outside of the group, differently coloured, peppered and salted, equally cavort-ing and skylarking, sometimes feeding, their mothers chuckling to them.

'They are not really lamas,' Oona was saying. 'See how the mothers feed them. They lie down.'

They not only lay down but stretched out their legs

and necks in a kind of mortal ecstasy, they curved round their heads to watch their feeding children in glorious attention. Oona got up and the whole herd seemed to be applauding at her interest and made way for her and one of the nursing mothers lay there and waited for Oona to approach her and the baby lama looked up from its feeding and did not seem to be afraid, and Oona stroked the mother and it stretched with a marvellous luxury. Oona found that she was only remembering when she used to feed Geoffrey, and those first times when Mycroft had watched her in a kind of wonder and had touched her breasts and her nipples with his fingers and his palm had become wet with her milk. Geoffrey so helpless in her arms.

Nicholas was contemplating. He looked back and up at that female figure crouched in stone above, its static subterranean oozing force a kind of high obscenity, vile only because it was out of scale, because coming out of the earth and giving birth back into it – it was an enormous dread. Gambolling between its knees these champagne thistle-down creatures, and here were more of them, they were lemon-coloured, the colour of good red wine or dappled or skewbald and now everybody was being urged to go with them, to leave the figure and to return to the flowers. Berenice being pulled by little teeth. Now they were all laughing and following them, Berenice and Nicholas holding hands, and the stone figure was behind them, waiting.

The lama was pulling her very gently by the skirt and she was laughing, and she only looked back once towards the figure and had just one distinct thought. Bruce would have worshipped it.

They were convoyed by all these tiny lamas. They stepped back into the gold of the forest, it was like leaving a place, like stepping into a different room. But there was not only the forest. There were the cliffs.

They were very near.

Berenice wondered why they called them cliffs. They had no top. Rather it was a wall, just as above these . . . trees? . . . there must be a ceiling. They had just come for a long walk.

Oona and Mycroft halted. The miniature lamas had scattered, had disappeared into the undergrowth as suddenly as they had appeared. The scuffling vanished away. They were alone with one another again and the forest was about them.

Why did they run away?

But the question passed quickly. At first it had been forgotten that this was a still place, a place without movement, of lofty columns and silent areas of coppered grass. The movement of stags, of unicorn, of boys racing under water, these only served to emphasize the incredible and empty stillness – like the cathedral that overbears with its emptiness the few tourists who are wandering about its body, being merely footfalls inspecting the arches and the tombs. Nicholas was filled with a sense of benevolent foreboding, an intuition that all this unmovement was about to sing like a bow.

The wall was much closer, overreaching their heads

and as they came under the final archway the effect of gold and light became muted by the sheer blue-grey.

'It's smooth,' Oona exclaimed.

It was made polished like some marble slab, and here the ground led quite sharply down towards it, towards a single opening.

'Our lift entrance,' Mycroft said.

He strode towards it, his stick in his hands. He heard the exclamations of the others, he saw that the gates were open. The lift was illuminated. It was fantastically as he remembered it. He felt a sudden unexpected emotional clutch, a connection to the remembered world it had come from. Now here it was again and as he came nearer he could see the long coffee-table. The elegant coffee-pot was steaming on its tile, there were four matching cups in mottled greys, each flicked with a spray of gold. There were four comfortable fireside chairs with soft tapestry cushions in blues and greens.

12

Mycroft could see right into the lift – there were even
two plates on that table each with a pile of fresh-cut
sandwiches, and between them was a large grey envelope.

Near the entrance to the once familiar gleaming
interior of the metal lift there was that same clump of
waxen scarlet elongated flowers. Standing beneath them,
its feet in the first position, was the creature. It was
observing their approach. It was still dressed as the
schoolgirl: the socks, the blouse, the beret set on the
cropped black hair, the precise neatness.

It did not say anything.

Mycroft looked at it in return, also without comment,
but he mused over the possibility that it might in fact
be the director of some calculated experiment, in spite
of the gymslip, of the smart precision of its uniform.
It was more likely that it was itself an instrument, a tool
chosen and contrived for a specific reason.

The imitation is almost perfect, Oona thought. She
looked at it, still wondering an old wonder – what would
it have been like to have had a girl child instead of
Geoffrey? Home would have had a differently tilted

centre of gravity – home? What home now? This was all there was.

'The lift is still here,' it said. 'It is quite capable of taking you – upstairs.' The brown eyes looked at them very steadily. It made no gesture of invitation, neither did it bar their way.

They all paused, almost guiltily, as if expecting it to say something further than this.

It was Mycroft who raised the technical point.

'But who will press the button to send us up?' He was remembering that there were no controls inside the lift.

'That can be taken care of,' it assured them.

They still watched, somehow certain that it was going to tell them some other thing.

It was speaking. There was the precisely brushed short black hair, the face that had been washed by coal-tar soap, the voice that spoke, that hardly seemed to speak from its mouth at all.

'But there is little likelihood of you actually wanting to ascend at present. It is enough for you to know that the means of leaving actually exist. If the means of leaving did not exist then you would not have any possible feeling of choice, and choice is to be one of the experiences that will happen to you. But first you are required to endure here. You will have to stay until you are both prepared and able to ask the right question. Until that moment, and we shall all know when that moment arrives, it is this place that you must try to understand.'

Oona watched the neat schoolgirl in front of them, the sweet expression, demure, polite. Yet with its hand it casually and uninhibitedly scratched its thigh while its voice continued with an almost unemotional ruthless instruction.

'Undisciplined indulgence, Brother Nicholas, without the framework of your community, it makes a heady drink, but it will be a drink that you will not be allowed to turn away. It will be difficult for you. And you, Doctor Oona Charrington, there will be no rushing off to help other people. Selfless service, that was an easy way out, but there is no one to help down here. Physical bliss is going free. You will find that you are cast back on your own resources. Nor, Mr Mycroft Charrington, will you be able to escape reality by turning everything you study into a neat set of abstract interrelations, into a pretty piece of mental meccano. You might get a booby prize for spotting some of the illogicalities down here. They have been built-in for your especial confusion. But now you have a more important occupation. You will have to begin to endure yourself.'

It was laughing at them.

'But you don't mention me,' Berenice said.

It stopped laughing but it still had a puckish smile.

'You will have to paint – without the benefit of an audience.'

Nicholas could hear the bell in the distance once more, a bell tolling.

It was Oona who spoke.

'So you think that now we have to be happy, Mycroft and I? You think that we have to give up everything we have ever had or known . . .?'

The creature shook its head.

'I am not concerned with you being merely happy. That is a relative thing. You have to learn to start with happiness, with having everything you ever wanted – and then to learn to go on from there.'

It looked hard at Oona, and then at Mycroft.

'I can make you happy – now. Deliriously happy. But before I do, can I remind you that this is only where you start from. Happiness, from your experience, from your culture, from what you have possessed, is only where you began. Happiness is not your question.'

It was a little girl again. It had a red ball in its hands and it was bouncing it, bouncing it with a great verve and eye and then it snatched it out of the air and threw it over their heads.

'Catch it, Geoff,' it shouted.

The red ball was thrown back.

The creature caught it very gracefully with an outstretched hand.

Geoffrey wearing the same shorts as he wore on holiday, still tanned, more tanned, barefoot, being greeted, greeting, laughing with them, at them, Mycroft knowing that you do not ask questions when you are joyful. At last Oona let him hug his son. Introductions, explanations, shyly shaking Berenice's hand, in wonderment at Brother Nicholas to Nicholas's amusement, a wonderful familiarity with the creature.

'She kidnapped me in the school cellars.'

and

'No, I just haven't been given the chance to be hungry down here, Mother.'

The two children playing with the red ball, the waxen scarlet elongated flowers, the illuminated lift that none of them went near. Oona saw the creature walk away from her son and turn round towards them.

'Perhaps it is the life down here that you have to face. The comfortable existence, the interesting and fascinating intelligent existence. There is nothing that you could do upstairs. A dying city, a dying country is no place for mock heroics. Your early death by radiation in a world without medical supplies will be neither a help nor a consolation to those whose deaths are already inevitable. You have other and more important matters to attend to. When you have asked the proper question – then you will be able to pass through those gates if you so wish.'

It stopped, quiet and confident and waiting for them. It exchanged glances with Geoffrey, as if Geoffrey was in on some secret, Geoffrey Charrington who was bouncing the rubber ball on the high blue cliff, the muscles of his brown bare flesh moving, co-ordinated and beautiful.

The golden light shone down from the roof, steady and yet perhaps less strong than a midday sun. Nicholas thought he could hear other bells now, not tolling but a carillon playing scales. He stood observing and listening from the safety of his habit, from behind the centuries of his order, seeing the obvious certainty and knowledge of the creature, virgin, child, so old, so morning-sprung.

'And when the moment arrives for our release,' Mycroft suggested, 'then your experiment will be complete?'

'No.' There was the remorseless voice again.

'The experiment will be complete when you ask the question, and the experiment is complete while you are waiting to ask the question, and again the experiment will be complete after you have asked this question and have made up your minds what you are going to do. This experiment is always complete – both at the beginning of time and during its time and after it has been completed – always.'

'But supposing,' Oona suggested, 'just supposing that we never do ask this question, supposing that we never stumble on it. Or supposing that we do in fact discover what this question is and we refuse to ask you. What will you do then?'

'But you will want to ask the question, Mrs Charrington, this is something that I know.'

'So this will be the point of the experiment,' Mycroft urged.

'It is all part of the experiment.'

'Then how do you know what the result will be?'

'I know the result already. It is you who are being made to make the experiment. It is you who have to experience the answer.'

'Then if this is an artificial experiment that you have set up then we cannot be certain that anything that you have told us so far – about ourselves, about what we are here for, about what has happened, is in any sense true. The conditions here may in fact be entirely artificial. This may only be a contrived laboratory.'

He could no longer see it as a little girl, as a schoolgirl

playing ball with his own son, he could only hear another mind answering his own.

'Nothing here is artificial. Everything here, as upstairs, is as it is. It is made that way. It is given. You could say that it will appear to follow certain rules. On the other hand you can never be certain. One is never certain about anything. One can only say that there are experiences that for oneself, for the time being, appear to be consistent. You have always had to take most things on trust. This was true of your lives before, although you did not often bother to question it.'

The boy and the girl, throwing, jumping and catching, their faces smiling, their hands grasping and casting the ball.

'But what are we supposed to do here?' Nicholas inquired.

'That is what I call the beginning of a real question,' it said. It was flushed a little from its exertions, it held the ball in its hands and would not throw it back. 'This place is here. You are inside it. Why do we have to have all these suppositions? The grass grows under your feet. How else should it grow?'

'So we have a certain liberty, the freedom of this place,' Oona suggested.

It said nothing. Geoffrey stood beside it. They stood side by side while it waited. There were the waxen and scarlet and elongated blooms just above their heads. Above them all the blue-grey cliffs rose sheer to the ceiling. Only Berenice looked back: huge grey-green arches and in the far distance the flash of a lake. Mycroft was talking again, quietly and reasonably, taking up a new point.

'If we are making this experiment then, then we must make our own investigations. If among many questions we must finally ask one question, then we must be free to examine, to compare, explore and discuss between ourselves.'

The creature nodded.

'You have to do what you must do. Now you may choose. I could tell you that all your choices are already made and have already been completed by what you are and what you know. Neither you nor I can avoid them. There is only your ignorance as to what your choice will finally be. Choosing is an experience.'

'And will you be with us?'

The creature looked away, stared far over and beyond their heads.

'I am always about,' it said softly. It was thinking.

'You may have to take the consequences,' it said.

'Consequences interest me.'

'The consequences will interest all of you. Consequences when recognized are a definition of what you call the real.'

Berenice swivelled her attention back towards the creature. She had been looking at the forest, at the formation of the feathery coppery leaves lying on the grass at her feet, at their vein structure, an affair of right angles, a most unnatural sight. She had been looking at Geoffrey standing and throwing. Even when they are so young there is this male stance, and she had tossed back her fair hair and had smiled at him, and he had registered her smile and had gone on bouncing his ball.

She would know when this question was asked correctly. Already, she could not formulate the question, but she *knew* its nature.

Berenice could remember that moment in the Lyons Tea Shop on the other side of Regent Street, downstairs, when Bruce had slouched over to her with his teacup (always tea – the only student of his year who never drank coffee) and Bruce had hardly ever spoken to her before and he sat down beside her, not opposite, sitting so close that his filthy jeans scraped along her leg.

'I've been looking at this thing that you're doing,' he had said finally. There had been a long pause before he had said that. Then he had just nodded. Bruce had drunk that tea in long deliberate mouthfuls to half-way down the cup. There was tea slopped in the saucer, there was cobalt blue on his thumb round the nail. The cup was put down.

'Not my sort of work,' he said. He was looking away from her. 'But it goes —'

The finger and thumb snapped.

'One, two, three, CLICK,' he said.

And he was still looking away from her, thinking, fascinating himself with the memory of her work, not really concerned with her as a girl at all. The dirty hand wrapped itself around the cup. He did not notice that she was beside him.

A quiet fell round them. Nicholas tried vainly to listen for the bells. Oona's hand caressed her son's bare shoulder.

'You will find me with you,' the creature was saying, 'while you make your observations. I may even present you with some of the evidence.'

'We shall have to look at everything that offers,' Mycroft interposed. 'Not merely what you show us.'

It grinned.

'You will only be able to examine what you want to examine, what you have the will to look at.'

It straightened its beret. Its feet were together.

'You have already said that you thought you found in me some sort of puppet manipulated by something else; or perhaps a key to a design, or a goddess, or just some new and as yet unexplained phenomena awaiting explanation. These were all quite valid suggestions. But now you are only permitted the simple scientist's observation. You may not like all you see. Some of your observations may prove to be banal, or too intimate, or too overwhelming. Nevertheless – you must watch. Watch again. Remember who you are. Remember that you will have to find out who I am, each in your own way. Remember that nothing is unimportant. You can only watch as closely as you can, for as long as you can bear.'

It became silent. The great grey-green archways seemed to Nicholas to have become stern. The copper-coloured grass curled round their feet. The polished wall of cliff rose like a vast blue backcloth.

It had kicked off its shoes. The neat beret was screwed up into a ball and flung into a clump of spiralling bending ferns. It was an animal now, an animal wearing a gym-slip and blouse. It played a little by itself. It paused, watching them to see what they might do. Then it did a private little pirouette. Its lips were grinning over its teeth.

'Come on, Geoff.'

The children were running round them, running back down in the lake direction, running back and round them.

They stopped.

It pointed to the lift. The gates were closed. They had not heard them.

'We are going this way,' the creature said.

The parents began to follow.

(But would Daddy and Mummy understand? This place was something that was his – this place was in no way theirs at all. Daddy always patiently explaining, Daddy always smiling – playing board games with one – 'Battle Royal' – a game of knights warring through Tewkesbury, Ludlow and Pomfret – Daddy always winning in a distant kind of way, his mind working elsewhere. Mummy always concentrated too hard and lost – if she wasn't called away on a case in the middle when Daddy took over. Dear Mummy always trying too hard. Though she was super with the Jag. But Daddy was the demon with the grey board and his coloured counters streaming in a ribbon of advance – St Albans to Hexham – and thinking elsewhere.)

The creature grabbed his hands.

The forest, Berenice noted, continued down before them. Now they walked over the copper grass and it was like traversing an immense sequence of ballrooms. A stepping bird, the importance of a gigantic turkey in a galaxy of purples and oranges trumpeted at their approach, stalked across their line of march, fluttered and danced to itself before a tree and then forgot that they were there. Berenice watched the movement of its colour.

Oona looked back. Already the lift gates were out of sight. Geoffrey and this creature running. Geoff was brown. A skewbald little lama galloped madly out about their feet, bleating excitedly and dashed back. The children paused to watch it, to wait for the others to catch up.

They tramped on.

Again they saw unicorn, nearer this time, tall brindled animals grazing, moving under the archways but slowly, looking at them with an immense curiosity but unalarmed. Smooth gentle beasts pausing, their great flanks flicking, their horns held high and upright or lowered to the pasture. Here they were existing.

Mycroft could see the lake again quite clearly. He picked at the soil with his stick.

It was not the facts of sex that Geoffrey had ever found difficult. As far as Mycroft could remember his mother had first told him. After all Oona was the doctor. But when they had all been walking along the Pembrokeshire coast one holiday Geoffrey had come out quite unexpectedly:

'But, Dad, do girls want you to do this to them when you make love?'

He remembered smiling a little.

'Why yes – girls want you to do this to them.'

'But – would a girl want me to do this to her?'

'Of course, if she liked you very much. Or she might want you to – do this out of curiosity. The sad thing about being young, Geoff, is that you cannot really know without experience, and you have this very natural ache to find out. But when you are really grown up, when you have done these things, you may be lucky enough to find out that it is not the thrill, nor the novelty of the something mysterious, or the something forbidden, that you are looking for. You will find that you make love to crown everything else that you do and share with this girl we are talking about.'

Pause.

'Do you and Mummy still make love?'

It was Oona who had chimed in, giving his hand a little squeeze, taking him off in his own words, his own tone of voice.

'Of course.'

Now Mycroft could hear Geoffrey's voice calling back to them: 'Is that your boat?'

And now the carillon was playing brightly, the sound much nearer. The punt was still waiting where they had left it. Nicholas felt a resumption of his former sense of intoxication, an unreasoning excitement and yet he knew that in spite of it he was at the same time feeling more at peace within, now that they seemed merely to be accepting this place and merely living here.

The creature turned a cartwheel, a flurry of plain white slip and girl's Marks and Spencer briefs. Then the monk found that it was looking at him, that they were exchanging glances, not speaking but both knowing . . . he could not express it in words, that was not required . . . they both understood at two different levels: at intoxication and sobriety.

Then he saw Berenice pointing to beyond the punt. The boys had returned and they were merely floating, drifting, just off-shore, honey-skinned and indolently lolling in the warmth. They took no notice of the approaching party, indeed they behaved rather like water-birds, chattering lazily between themselves and paddling a little farther away as they were approached. They seemed to be waiting.

Berenice felt an urge to take up her sketch-book, to sit, to look, to absorb, to be alone with all these surroundings. It flowed from the certainty that to draw, that to reproduce the things she saw was also a sure way to master them.

The long sheet of green water reached outward and away from them, a still mirror under the vast and reaching archways. They would all get into the punt, they would float, they would drift away onwards and slowly. Already Mycroft and Nicholas were edging the boat back into the water. Geoffrey was the first to jump in, then Oona. A large crimson heron stalked fastidiously through the shallows, inspecting all those present with a certain prim attention. A yellow tortoise, yellow as lemons, stumped indifferently by, moving at legal speed. Mycroft saw a spotted fox. Geoffrey half looked away for the creature was straddling modestly over a mass of kingcups, gym-slip hitched high and functioning almost boy-fashion, charming, oblivious and public. An orange kingfisher flashed over their heads, banking and wheeling through black blossom. They waited.

'She would,' Geoffrey thought.

'Come on,' Berenice called at last.

It bounded into the punt with them. Mycroft suggested that they should go in the opposite direction to the house. Nicholas pushed off. Everybody was comfortable.

Lazily they proceeded, crossing between the lily pads, blue and gold dragonflies quivering and swaying, hanging before their eyes, sliding horizontally away – left – ascend. The punt's progress became a gradual motion following the gentle tide.

'We are intoxicated,' Brother Nicholas remembered, as he pushed very slowly on his pole. 'We do not need to be resisted, we eat of the lotus and the time is always early afternoon.'

'How far does the wall go back?' Mycroft inquired.

The creature sat between him and Geoffrey, its knees clasped to its chin, seemingly in a dream.

'How far would you like it to go back?'

Mycroft remembered that he must ask his questions of himself. He stretched out his feet in the bottom of the punt. Oona and Geoffrey were hanging over the side, looking at fishes. He could see, walking between the trees, a vast and woolly elephant with rust-red hair. It walked delicately, it was, he supposed, a mammoth, and suddenly it raised its trunk and, standing on the lake's edge, trumpeted. They were startled. It was a weird and mournful note. The trunk was twisted back in salutation. Their own creature raised an august hand in dignified acknowledgement.

A cloud of vermilion butterflies whirled round the great shaggy head. It turned heavily away.

Suddenly they seemed to be surrounded by an immensity of activity. Humming-birds, flits of colour, were darting across their bows in contra directions. With a kind of mechanized onrush boys were passing under again, spewing bright bubbles and streaming, turning on their backs this time as if to look upwards at them, frothing and propelling, diving under water-plants, surfacing and laughing. A gathering of snow-pink flamingo were walking outwater with dignity where a group of girls were skylarking down, a shaggy wolf running with them, girls coloured yet platinum, fuzzy-haired and mongol-eyed, furry and splashing and bounding, the wolf chuckling, the beat of wings as black swans off-surfaced, lifting above them. Oona saw a small white bear drinking. Butterflies! Butterflies!

'Look, look,' Geoffrey was urging.

Nicholas and Berenice had seen it before, the great column of water falling from the high gold roof above them, falling without apparent motion and soundless on to the lake's still surface, ice still against the distant confusions of blossoms, the bunched fruit in offerings. But this time there was a difference, for they could all see that while the water should be falling it was in reality drawing upwards, and as they came nearer they suddenly saw the group of swimming boys project through into the column, driving powerfully and vertically up through its centre, blowing rainbows from their mouths, rising like tiny fishes, a spasm of impelling onrush jerking roofward. The touch of feathers – white doves wheeling about the water column – a cascade rising. Now also there was the gambolling of animals, spotted hounds pirouetting, great tongues lolling, the bleatings of tall sheep blue-fleeced like blue smoke between trees advancing, the desperate overhead wedding clangour of bells.

Geoffrey standing erect.

And the stealing sense of all things below, rodent feet, silken whiskers, bright eyes exploring, the insistent impossible intrusion into the silent heap of the granary, the gentle mice of paradise scurrying and golden in their fine-worked burrow, soft feet caressing dark undergrowth.

They felt held by their spines to their boat.

Go up! Go up! Go up!

An agonized sense of hesitancy, of waiting after the final moment of decision, of holding back when a return is no longer possible, a terrible halt before the gates are thrown open to the uttermost patience and understanding: but the voice of Mycroft in their ears, the steady level and continuing voice:

'I know that this is neither the question nor the answer. We have first to do our own asking and we must make our own answer. We will not be stampeded. We do not disregard what we see, we accept it, but now we must for the present, turn away. TURN US ABOUT, Brother Nicholas, we go no farther here. This too – but not this only.'

Nicholas did not know why but he had found himself toiling to send the punt onwards, the flapping of colour before him, humming-birds brighter and brighter, the great mammoth advancing into the water, the wolf with scarlet jaws and the girl's thigh deep and advancing and himself desperately poling . . .

'Turn us about, Nicky.'

Nicholas saw the face of Mycroft Charrington looking anxiously up towards him; he saw Berenice, lips parted, rigid and staring at the great elephant, Oona half-rising trying to dissuade Geoffrey from diving and everything swayed and then a bank of mist rolled across them and suddenly he was transfixed, feeling the punt only under his feet and not seeing it and having no directions, no birds and silence only. Everything was grey and neutral and he was sober and a dank chill was round him. There was no roof, no light, he had to search for his own hands.

'I have mercy.' Its voice was gentle in his ear.

He felt the creature take the pole from him. It had a powerful grip. He knew they were turning. They were escaping. Nothing could stop their regress. It braced itself beside him and pushed.

Mist was swirling round them. At moments he was a little clearer. Grey shapes of trees were glimpsed and then they faded. They were poled. He did nothing. At moments he could see the others, grey shapes huddled beneath him, at moments the water. There was once a splash and a swirling and what might have been one of the girls or perhaps an otter went swiftly by and then the mist closed over them again. The creature was still poling.

At moments he felt he would step out into a vacuum, off the punt, out into nothing. They were being poled into a waiting eternity.

Mycroft had stopped thinking. He was gripping Geoffrey, Oona. Something else was to happen. All at once he realized that the house was above them, that they were sliding up to the landing-stage. Vaguely the mist was parting but they could see little.

Someone had tied up. They were led up and inside, into the main part of the house.

The lights were on. (Lights? What lights? There was light.) They walked into a yellow glow and a tea was laid on a white tablecloth, the pot just filled, a large brown motherly English pot of good tea, muffins and a plum cake sliced and opened, one of Berenice's pictures almost familiar on the wall.

It was Oona who began to put milk in the teacups, while they vaguely arrived, milled round her, sat down bewildered. Nicholas contemplated them going through familiar motions – the continuation of habit after the extraordinary. It was Geoffrey, who had never been here before, who pointed out the one thing that was different since they had left. Set against one wall was a large grey table-sized cabinet, spread with a dust cover, and from which a mass of coloured cables ran out to the wall.

'What's this thing?' Mycroft asked the creature, but the creature was helping itself to plum cake.

13

The glitter of light on the spines of old volumes, on the deep leather-bound tomes; or on slim new books with sombre brilliant dust-covers – books where the authors were all unknown, books that wanted to be read by the fingers, books that impart a tactile enjoyment when the pages turn. There are books which fascinate, because there are maps, endpapers, pockets from which maps can be outspread, maps and charts of unvisited countries, plans of cities as yet unbuilt, all marked with the routes travellers might have taken. There were books here with pictures, wide books with colours so intense that unless one looked out of the window one could not believe in the picture's possibility. There were also books that had only been bound in paper, but each boasted a picture on its cover, each picture is different, a furry animal in a basket, a girl with bare breasts. On these shelves there were books with empty pages and books with pages that were holed like windows in a house so that one could see the pages that were to come. There were books that were old friends, the scent of familiar print and honest binding, books that pleased by memory but were no more read. There were books that were not only read, but were handled, stacked, brought down and loved.

Books are an encoded perishable record of some corner of eternity. Within the confines of each book the reader has the eye of God.

Chairs in a comfortable library where there is now no hurry to finish because there is time without ambition, desire without haste, understanding without the need to remember.

The possibility of looking up from what you are reading to looking out through the various windows: at intervals darkness descends on the high forest. There is the illusion of time. Outside the windows, when one deigns to look, there is an assortment of weathers; mostly the diffused and imitation sunshine, sometimes a winter, sometimes obscuring mist blanketing the outlook with an obtuse and blessed silence, sometimes a warm and enveloping rain with a display of serried rainbows in endless multicoloured lanes. Often there were distant children running through the showering water and once – a prancing hippogriff.

Receive: an absence of problems. The mechanics of life are carefully provided for, the method is undisclosed. The subjects are only haunted by the curious efficiency, the departure of soiled clothes, the tube of toothpaste that is always full, the changing selection of ties that Mycroft can always find.

A present for Geoffrey: the grey table-sized cabinet, glass-topped, illuminated, into which one can look down. This miniature biological place, an aquarium full of intertwining growths through which complex cell creatures perambulated, twisted, fed and absorbed, mated, split, redivided, intimately rejoined, became one, became as new. Nobody knew what they were except that they were Geoffrey's. He watched them.

He could turn a switch.

There would be an alteration in the environment, an alteration within certain defined and apportioned limits. A change in the environment brought an alteration in the behaviour, in the growth, mobility and capacity. This has an infinite interest. One can proceed: manipulation, change, observation, the satisfied recognition of a familiar routine, the titilation of the unexpected; all in a private glass case – this spells 'pleasure' or that more acceptable word 'satisfaction'.

There is no hurry.

One is content.

Consider the creature.

Here, one might suggest, is a special case. For the moment, however, let us put aside this aspect for it depends upon your level of judgement, the angle of your observation, the time at which you choose to intervene in the process. Remember that mere observation alters and interferes, not only with the object that is being seen, but also with the subject that conducts the examination.

The creature is staying with them now. As with Geoffrey it has its own bed, its own chair, its place at table. Geoffrey accepts it on its face value, as a companion, a girl with unusual ways in what is an unusual place, another person in the house – as his age against the adults.

Berenice spends time drawing the creature, drawing Geoffrey, boy and girl together or apart – or as it. The pencil of Berenice tracing endlessly over huge sheets of paper as if to find in the shapes and contours of their animal bodies some hint of the question that was sought. She watched them swim, she reproduced their characteristic movements, textures, reflections, she observed. But here, gradually and now, as she dived in to swim with them as she sometimes did, what she had seen vanished, disappeared in the joy of her own swimming, of the warm green water sliding along her limbs. To paint, to draw into her own pictures her own freedoms, the moment that the green water closes over one's head, the moment when she sits on the bank squeezing her pale hair and there is no hurry and she is content with the ducks passing. Here is the moment of contentment when the creature and Geoffrey frolic in the lake together, when they both sit and lie on the landing-stage with their legs dangling, the warm light on their brown skins. To be aware at last that there was no need to record, no need to suggest their shapes, shades and movements, to suggest her own thoughts, feelings, reactions about what she saw, what she remembered, what she deduced. Here and in this place was a sufficiency.

The boy Geoffrey looked at her sometimes – shyly, interested, young and male. But in this place she did not feel herself to be a temptation, an unkind frustration, she sat on the bank among the blue and yellow poppies

167

and stretched out and let him gaze his full – she too was an extension of this endless omnilateral contentment.

The boy would return to his aquarium, watching endlessly through his own eternity of time.

The creature continued.

Berenice was recalling an occasion at the flat. She had spent the day painting a girl friend, a long girl stretched along her half-made bed and Bruce had been mooching around maintaining them, pushing cups of tea in their direction at regular intervals, amusing Rosie when she got bored, cooking up baked beans and making toast. Bruce was always very long-suffering, very intelligent, especially when trying to get his own way.

'My God, that makes it go one, two, three, click, Rosie.'

Berenice had been well aware that from Bruce's point of view the whole object of the exercise, the whole object of the day, was to get Rosie to go while leaving herself, Berenice, in a happy, positive and receptive mood. She had, as it happened, been quite content with the prospect of Bruce being here at the flat all evening, but it must be not just yet. In the meantime, in the middle of his antics, Bruce was often worth listening to. Besides she got a lot more done while he was there to fix the food.

'It's not a matter of feeling and seeing something. You have got to – hell you've got to know it's significant, that it's got value – for you. Otherwise you are not living at all. How would I explain? Well it's a bloody sight better to contemplate a beautiful woman than to be one. Sometimes, when you make, love you wish at the same time that you could just stand at the other end of the room, so that you could really see and know who it is you are loving.'

But do I agree? Berenice reflected. Sometimes one did wish that he would stand at the other end of the room. Bruce was always so hot. Yet when one was painting, and when Bruce was painting, one did, he did, stand back, one did contemplate. But then one tried and tried to sense the moment of being inside the thing, the moment of going up to it and into it, the moment when one surrounded it oneself. Both things must be remembered.

Dear Bruce – do you go one, two, three, click, now?

Would he have liked this place, where the contemplation, the being, the work, all seemed to be one?

Nicholas prayed.

He prayed neither desperately nor vainly, but with a professional certainty, following a precise and well-tried procedure through recollection, silence and contemplation, each stage, each mental gesture in its own time and in its own place in patience and waiting. He was aware that what they were all seeking could emerge only from themselves, but that this knowledge must be discovered by each individual for himself. The message could not possibly be told.

The Prior had stood tall and stooped in the garden. There was a place where one could look outwards across the island and contemplate the sea. But he had his back turned towards the view. Father Prior was an attentive gardener but he preferred the wild things best. He was touching, feeling with his finger the lichen on the dour stone wall, feeling with his finger the tenacious springy surface of the living thing. Brother Nicholas remembered himself watching, the Prior was never hurried, often eccentric in the sense that he was always seeing the right thing in a new way.

'I am often amused by human beings,' he said. It had been a day when there had been a great many visitors to the monastery and the monastery gardens. 'They come here, not knowing what they are looking for – an afternoon's amusement, a day out for the children – and then not a few of them sense that there is something here that has value. They glimpse what perhaps they hardly knew they were looking for and they do not know exactly what it is. They are unable to identify it. They have seen, very briefly, something of the outward form of our life. We know that it is necessary. We love it. Often we love it too much. But that in itself is not the point of our community. It only creates it. It is this moment rather, this now, between bells, between labours, between worship and prayer even, when we are sometimes given the grace to know what we have. This is the moment when the cake is both eaten and preserved, the moment when we sit unguilty in the garden before the apple is eaten.'

Nicholas could recall pulling up his big Massey tractor, his habit hitched up round him, beckoning the visitors to cross his path. They smiled at him, the flowery frocks and the men's self-conscious holiday shirts, the bags and the bottles. He had nodded at them and smiled in return. May God bless them and it was good to tow the rank manure up the steep rutted track. The scent of work, the effort of his own stubby hands, the certainty that he was depended upon.

Today he had been idling on his bed, watching Oona ironing smalls, her own and Berenice's and the children's. She had developed a need to launder herself.

Nicholas had seen Berenice praying in the chapel and had tip-toed by. The candles burning, the presence of the host, the ultimate presence waiting for all time, the creature putting its tongue out across the altar, Mycroft standing in the background, quite silent . . .

An impelling curiosity to watch the bathroom, to watch it all day; just to see what exactly changed the soap and the hand towels. (The soap was always new, the towels were always clean!) Curiosity is a twentieth-century virtue.

'But would you really be any happier if you knew how it worked?' the creature asked with a smile.

Nicholas was distracted for a moment. When he turned back the towels and the soap were . . . presto!

Conjuring was fun.

Miracles are not necessary to true knowledge.

Ask Mycroft:

'Would you really be happier if you knew how it worked?'

'I would imagine that I would think I was happier.'

The suffocating silent excitement, seated alone at his desk over his large sheets of squared paper, the excitement hardly contained when he perceived a pattern in his work-team's results. Here, contained in figure and pattern of statistic the patient end of four years painstaking re-testing, breeding and development. Funds, equipment, immaculate premises, official encouragement. He remembered the effort he had to resist the temptation to rush out and show his colleagues. But he held to the better way. They must, like himself, perceive the information in its new setting, they must recognize the pattern, reach through for themselves to this new conclusion, as he had arrived there. They must understand from the feet up. But he must sit now, he must keep their triumph in perspective, this triumph that could of course never be published. Eric, Elvira, Josh Waterman, Doctor Cuthbertson – only yesterday they had all been discussing the deadlock in the programme, all together at lunch, the endless urgent talk over the sunshine pudding and custard. And now, so soon, this marvellous success. Perhaps it would now be true to say that England had the means to infect the world at will with a galloping leprosy, more swiftly, more certainly than they had ever hoped, than they had ever been able to offer before. It was a pity that the elegant Charrington-Cuthbertson effect would have to remain a secret.

The creature asleep over a book, to be horizontal, to be absolutely unconscious, that too seemed to be a particular wisdom – the stillness beyond the windows, the stillness over the lake surface.

Mycroft's fingers moved over his suit, crawling and feeling, looking for the answer to the question that he could not remember.

Oona is still magnificent, a splendid woman when she moves. She watches her husband thinking, her mind busily exploring, registering, trying to understand what even now, after all these years of living with him, it is still not quite possible to discern in someone other than oneself.

There is Geoffrey – playing with his toy.

She ponders her best death.

The fat German Baroness, not a child, a private patient, and the Baroness had liked her. Helga Welt had known for some time that her visits to Doctor Charrington were only because she was in search of a slightly postponed, a rather more comfortable end. Some of her visits had been made quite simply (and they had both known it) to purchase a conversation. Oona had also realized that the conversation was truly between the Baroness and her own self. The doctor was only the public, the audience of one. She spoke an excellent clipped English.

'When I was a little girl in Saxony, even then I was fat, I wrote poems I told no one about, because I enjoyed walking, walking over the sand-dunes, discovering that I was alone, that I was myself thinking. You know what I mean? Yes? I was first myself there by the German coast, a little fat *mädchen* sucking a piece of grass. Behind that grass I thought. I went home, I made poetry about what I had discovered. It was a poetry to me. Yes! The poetry fixed the experience. Other people did not know. It was my treasure. Afterwards I grew fatter, I studied in Heidelberg, I even fell in love – and he surprised us both by marrying me. I still wrote about philosophy, I was myself and I attended many conferences, I asked questions. The mind revolved. Often my husband was surprised that I so existed, just as he was surprised that he should die before me.'

Helga Welt would pause now. To converse and simultaneously to ignore the reality of her own body had always been some effort and it was now the supreme effort. 'She' was somewhere inside.

'My mind, Dr Charrington, it still likes to walk over that sand. It sucks that grass. It is amused, even now, when looking down over the comedy of this body. But the true treasure, the one certainty, that is oneself.'

And she died. Oona was called in and there was nothing left to do. Her rooms had been lined with books, papers were everywhere, the proofs of her last book, the notes for a new project in an old exercise book. The people who lived with her were sorry for her.

'They should have envied,' Mycroft heard his wife say. 'Only last week she was asking me about her own body's run down, describing her symptoms, fascinated by facts and explanations, seeing a point and telling me before I could explain it myself. Her last words to me were: "It will be made into a poem." She was a real aristocrat.'

The creature asleep over a book, the girl-child sleeping, charming, absolutely unconscious, bliss incarnate, a girl-child asleep: yet watching, lidless, unwaking, perpetual: the unchanging merciful observation.

Overhead, far above the domes of the house, the golden reaching archways racing upwards in leafy metallic tracery. A bat, great arms outstretched, hanging in space, hanging to swoop.

The creature drinking tea, making tea for them, padding comfortably round them, listening, joining in their conversations a little, being in the background, chasing Geoffrey, being chased by him.

'For goodness' sake, children,' Oona said.

Far ahead, beyond the creature, the distant coppered fields, rising one by one in a great staircase, a great congregation of white stags moving, a torrent of huge beasts in migration.

The question . . . coagulating, ordering like a foetus borne in separate minds, not to be spoken, expressed or described, the creature observing. The question growing in miniature, a division of reforming and complexifying cells and ramifying systems. Unbeknown to them the creature saw the question they were looking for already asked in their minds and asked repeatedly.

All things are already contained within the volumes, facts, diagrams, maps that are to be laid out, intimate illustrations for the scholar; a book of smells, odours fragrantly greeting when the finger moves, turning the blank impregnated pages. A long row of green tomes on a high shelf that have only to be opened – when the librarian brings to hand the right volume. But the library is always complete. The book is always there.

The creature sitting at the top of a tall ladder, gloriously reading.

14

I sit reading. I am watching the words, the pictures, the quality of the sounds. I feel sweat in the hair of the arm-pit, warmth between the legs, the toes in a shoe. I sit in my place observing through girl's eyes. I am not a girl. They all sit round the girl, Oona, Berenice, Geoffrey, Brother Nicholas, Mycroft. I am not a man, not a boy. They are my tentacles, the ends of my antennae, the whorls in my ear, the tip of my tongue touching flesh, the pupil of my eye. Without them I do not speak, without them I do not eat tonight, except for their eyes I am blind.

To be Infinite is to be nothing.

'Let there be light – and there was light. Also, and for the first time, there I saw my shadow. We had begun.'

For the infinite the true pleasure lies in not knowing, in being unable to realize what is to come next, in not seeing what lies beyond the hill. Ignorance is for me: the miracle.

And then ... through you I want to know – all over again.

Geoffrey eating an apple, young teeth on apple flesh, Geoffrey wondering.

I am reading. You will notice that I do not read the last chapter of a detective novel first.

But you, whom we love so dearly, you pick the book up for me and you do not know.

Sometimes it is a problem to be a strong brown God.

I am immobile. I am in all places.

I am reading.

The girl is speaking. I speak.

'You have asked yourselves – although you have had what you want (you have been successful in your careers, you have never been hungry) although you have peace now, you still ask yourselves what it is that you still want. Recognition? There is no one to recognize you now. To go back? Do you want to go back to the misery of death that you have so firmly inflicted on yourselves? No, it was not the Russians, nor the Americans, nor the French, nor the Chinese – they too are yourselves. Do you wish to expiate the guilt for your small parts in allowing it to happen by trying to understand why you should do these things? Do you wish to help just one dying victim, to bind up just one child that he may know pain for just a little while longer? Do you wish to record the ultimate horror of an immediate human agony so great that there is neither the time nor the capacity to contemplate this end to a culture so proud, so full, so civilized, so helpless? It will make a fine picture, the great scar that is London. There has been nobody to date to record the shapes, to paint the searing and unusual colour of this original decomposition. Or do you perhaps wish to hear just one little man's irrelevant babbling confession, before he leaves you, that he too was once unfaithful to his kindly wife (and she is now dead)? No, you do not want any of these things. These are the worst things in the world, for all England has now become that certain room, Room 101, the place where one is summoned to the reality that no one can bear, the particular truth that each of you will be unable to face. These are not the things that you want. But although you are fed, although you are warm, although you are successful, although you are at peace – yet still you are not satisfied. Peace alone is not enough. You know, far far back in the rearmost corner of your minds a certain doubt. You each have a question – you still have a want. Tell me.'

It was Mycroft Charrington who spoke, who replied gravely to the innocently alarming little face.

'But supposing that we know what we want – would it be given to us?'

It wrinkled its nose. It nodded.

'This is the next stage in the experiment. Let me explain. Whatever you want, you shall have. Ask, and you shall receive.'

They were silent.

'Ask anything,' it insisted. 'You will find it the biggest responsibility of all – freedom – the ability to have what you want.'

They stood there in a row: Oona, Mycroft, Geoffrey, Berenice, Brother Nicholas.

'But there is one single condition – you are *bound* to choose.'

They possessed nothing here, except their clothes, their firm bodies, their knowledge and experiences, their quiet new-found, now almost taken-for-granted friendships, and the view through the glass walls of the house, the view of the golden leaves and the lake with the swimming children, the unicorn and the distant deer moving: the ultimate peace.

And their desires.

The creature was waiting without hurry and without impatience. It looked first at Berenice.

The fair girl's tongue came out between her lips as she spoke.

'But I have always had what I want – outside. I've never known what it is to be without – oh, the shapes and the sounds and the excitement of feeling and tasting. Even when I was a little girl – once when it was snowing, I went into the garden, I took off my shoes, Mummy was furious. I went and stood in the snow. It was just there. Mummy made me come in at once. But I couldn't put snow on to my white paper. I couldn't repeat that freezing melting wetness up between the toes, I couldn't bring that out on my paper. It's like seeing a bell, its shape and roundness and yet not being able to clang yourself. Or to hear it toll and not to be able to cast its shape. So you work, you try to reach skills, you draw, you sing, but still you have not yet got the confidence to let go, to let all happen without yourself, to let the shape of the bell come from you, to let the sound come out of you, to let the white of the snow well up between your toes. But down here, what I see, what I hear, is somehow brighter, more intense, more overwhelming – and so you have more self-consciousness to throw away, more suspicion about your own inadequacy. I don't want more of anything – I want to be able to take more. Can I ask for that?'

'You have asked for it,' the creature acknowledged, sucking its thumb. 'You have only to wait for your friends. What do you want, Mycroft Charrington – what do you want instead of that?'

Mycroft looked down thoughtfully at the brown face, at the incredible age of its youth.

'What do I want here?' he asked slowly. He did not look at her, he looked at his fingers, his palms. 'I think I want – will you understand what I mean – a table to stand on. I find that in living here nothing yet fits. I see creatures. I see plants. I am not certain that they are creatures. I am doubtful if they are plants. It is like seeing a great distance and then putting out your hand and thrusting a fist through it. I am excited, like Berenice, by what I see, what I find, excited and frightened. But I don't want more things that I cannot understand. I want to be able to have a table of understandings where I can start from in the same way as I need a vista of unknowns to investigate. Here too much is not quite known, too much lacks sense. I really want *fewer* things than I have, but I do want some of those things to fit – to make a platform, a table.'

'I understand you,' the creature said. It turned its stare on Brother Nicholas.

Nicholas gazed back.

'I am not satisfied with this place,' he replied evenly. 'I am grateful but not satisfied. Through us you watched our world – you watch this one. Do not think that I am afraid of comfort, I can manage that. Do not think that I am afraid of idleness. That too could be discovered in a monastery. There are times when one must be prepared to endure an idle and comfortable existence. But you do not give me any choice. Do not imagine that I think hard work in itself a virtue, or discipline an end in itself. These virtues too are only the temptations of the monastery. But I want to be able to choose between them. You do not allow me that down here. You ask me if I want to hear one little man's irrelevant confession before he dies. I do not want to hear his agony but I want to be able to help him in his suffering. For it is you that babbles that confession, just as you are his wronged wife, and it is you who in me will hold his hand and listen with me to his words. Is it you who fear Room 101? Or are you, through me, foolhardy enough to go back up inside the lift again? If you ask me what I want – I want to go back and try. You say that I shall have what I want and you ask me. My answer may not be the right one but it is mine.'

'I am not judging your requests,' it assured him. 'I do not judge at all. I am all your causes. I have given you your reasons. When you judge them I can offer you mercy but your answer is your answer.'

It turned towards Dr Oona Charrington. She felt

somehow insufficient with her own answer, too simple, too obvious. She stood there just hearing the words come out of her mouth.

'I only want our old world,' she said softly. 'The place that is familiar, that we have always known, the place in which we have grown with the people who for better or for worse, have grown with us. There is a Nigerian woman at my dairy who tells me about her daughter at Cambridge, a sensible woman dimly trying to grasp at what molecular chemistry might mean. There is our plumber who digs up history under the pipes of Isleworth and tells me what he understands about his finds while he changes my tap. Give him a cup of tea and he will give you back a lifetime. We have relations we love and relations we hate, the friends who have let us down and the neighbours who make us laugh, and the other ones that we cannot quite fathom – and when we go back. . . .' For a moment her voice broke off, she looked the creature straight in the face: 'But when we go back I shall want to remember, to know and to continue to know, what we know now, what we have seen here, what has happened to us since we have come downstairs.'

The creature squatted on its heels, its chin in its hands.

'That might be,' it conceded, 'a little more difficult, but I expect it could be managed.'

There was only Geoffrey left.

'What do you want, Geoff?'

He was smiling. He produced the red ball from his pocket.

'CATCH.'

It made a prodigious leap and snatched the ball out of the air. As it sprang the light, the scenery, the world beyond the walls vanished into darkness. Only the house, empty, only themselves standing inside it, remained in light. The creature was standing, was magnified, projected upwards so that it was for a single moment vast, a living torso reaching high into the dome, its own eyes closed and sightless, while an owl outstretched, befeathering its loins, benignly stared. Then the creature itself smiled, as if wires were pulling, were manipulating lips. The hips hinged, the body bowed.

'To hear is to obey. To ask is to receive. To want is to have.'

As it is written in the book, so it is written.

15

Light, a shadowy suggestion of light reflected on leaves high above the head, a pleasant easeful pinking rose-touched light that left everything without any particular definition. Not the light of the sun but rather the light of an enormous auditorium – HOUSE LIGHTS– UP! Here was an auditorium that was a great outside.

One did not bother to look, to look comprehendingly, not yet.

The creature was in shorts, khaki shorts and a shirt with breast pockets, even with khaki socks and heavy boots. It was opening a tin.

Berenice closed her eyes again. She could not remember going to sleep – she was only aware of this rather blissful awakening. Warm moss-like cushioning was under her head, her back, her feet. Everything gave. Something hummed, hummed, went away and then returned, a furry insect singing round her head.

'Where are we?' she heard Mycroft's puzzled voice inquire.

He too awoke comfortable in body, stretched out on sweet-smelling moss. (Tarragon? his mind wondered. Not quite but nearly tarragon, his mind decided.) Something tiny walked respectfully over his hand. He did not brush it off. He opened his eyes.

Now everything was filled with light. Away over his feet was a bright copper-coloured meadow flickering with light, and beyond and below a whole stairway of meadows leading down and down. Far in the distance he could see another glint, far below on the valley floor, a bubble on a mirror, the bubble house upon the lake. They were outside. They had travelled. The roof was not so far away.

'We have come to grant your wishes,' the creature announced. 'We have to grant them somewhere.'

Berenice lazily opened her eyes and stretched. Perhaps they had been camping. A fire was crackling at the creature's feet. There was a rich and overflowing scent of coffee.

'Where's Oona got to?' Mycroft asked looking all round, not seeing her and so not seeing anybody.

'Having their wishes granted,' the creature explained, now carefully pouring milk into a saucepan. 'It's just that their wishes had to be granted in a different place.'

Mycroft digested this piece of information.

'Do you mean to tell me that she's by herself . . . somewhere?'

'She is not by herself,' the creature said, balancing her saucepan on the fire. 'Nicholas is with her and I am with her. That's where they wanted to go.'

'But you're here with us,' Berenice pointed out.

'And there,' the creature said firmly. 'Two places at once I'm afraid, but don't keep pointing it out. It makes Mycroft uncomfortable.'

Mycroft Charrington did not hear it. He liked Oona at breakfast time. Oona not being there was like having a stranger in the house. The flood of light and morning well-being seemed to drop in tone with the discovery that she was absent. He supposed that Geoffrey was with Oona too.

'What do we do when we have had our wishes granted?' he asked grumpily.

The creature busied itself with its cooking. ('Don't look at the scenery, Berenice, that makes *you* uncomfortable. Grab a plate.')

'All your wishes will be granted, both spoken and un-spoken, whether you like it or not. Do you think that I don't know what they are? But your spoken wishes will be granted first. You do not have to trust me. You do not even have to have faith in me. I am here and come what may I shall take you both by the scruff of the neck and give you what you want, even if you don't know what it is that you do want.'

The creature said no more. Berenice was silent. Mycroft's hands trembled as he ate but the creature made him eat. There was a steady supply of sausage and bacon and toast and butter and more coffee.

The house-lights were coming up in full, a whole panorama of the forest stretched out and below and around them as if they were on a hill. A party of ant-eaters shambled up in their tired baggy trousers, nosing and licking, having a lust for English marmalade, rubbing their heads against knees. A yellow rat sat disconcertingly upon the creature's shoulder, accepting sausage and preening whiskers. Big parti-coloured squirrels went gliding overhead, flying squirrels tobogganing through the air like boys in furry skirts to land and then come waddling back, all looking as if they were wearing housecoats just a size too large. Mycroft had little appetite and the squirrels helped him out.

Colours glowed, changing and intermixing through the roof above their heads with a kind of bubbling sparkling unexpected gaiety. The animals gambolled a little, ate a small amount and then sat on the sidelines to watch the visitors eat. Two meadows below a herd of pure white cattle spread themselves to graze. Berenice found herself laughing quietly inside. They all looked outwards down the vistas of this world. Even Mycroft felt himself to be invaded by an impossible cheerfulness that ached only because Oona was not here to share.

A collection of girl children came by, more like decorations than persons, Berenice decided, but they removed the left-overs, the rubbish of breakfast, and went off chattering, yet not talking to the creature, let alone themselves. They disappeared, a jingle of laughter, flowers in the hair, their kilts swinging as they ran.

'Do we have our wishes granted now?' Mycroft inquired.

It looked at them. It stood up, shooing the rat away. It wiped its mouth on a large white handkerchief.

'Come on,' it said, 'now for the end of the journey.'

They began to climb.

This is an end without a beginning, Berenice thought. Normally she hated the ends of journeys, the boat-train from Folkstone after two months with Bruce in Crete, the sudden prospect of splitting up again, the separate flats and the separate work. Bruce never wanted to change. Bruce was always more ambitious than herself. This was his life. This was her playing it. Or the over-firm comfort of one of those faintly surrealist airway buses, growling along the motorway after the last plane from Amsterdam, back to the British advertisements in the sodium lighting, the yellow glow over empty streets. Midnight gone and the suburbs are tucked into their beds. Only the big lorries steaming west: Cardiff, Barnstaple, Hereford and Gloucester, tomato high and nationalized, a hot night and big men driving in their vests, the headlights floating in her eye. The flat would be clock-stopped, silent and musty from shut windows. A milkless home where one is too tired to sleep, kept awake by new impressions of the over-familiar.

They had come to the edge of the meadow. A little cliff, fifty feet, Mycroft reckoned, made a step up to the next level. There was a narrow goat path leading up the side, up over the almost transparent blue rock. The creature ran up. It was almost dancing.

'Will it be worth seeing?' Mycroft wondered, turning automatically to help Berenice. (It was Oona his mind was helping.) The creature was already far above them, sitting way up at the top and taking off its boots. The dark hair of the creature, the head looking down, the brown eyes looking carefully at him. They were reaching the end of their journey?

'Stop thinking,' Mycroft whispered into his head. The

instruction to himself. No, he would not consider any immediate possibilities. (What you shall want you shall have. Ask and you shall receive.)

The mice huddling together, long pink tails, the bodies breathing. The rustle of tiny bodies in plastic litter. To drink from a saucer of water, to be lifted up, to be marked by a minute coloured ring, the exploration of a small nose, the sensation of a whisker. To mate with a quivering she-mouse, to be a she-mouse mated, a tiny enveloping lust. To be infected with a calculated death, two days, three days – the body on its back, the small rodent mouth open, the fact noted by the girl in the dark hair looking down. Here were the precise white overalls. Three generations, thirty, three hundred, chosen to die – that row of observation cages in the south aisle. After the third day – the survivors, if any, will be noted. From a series of these observations it is possible that a man, that men, women and children may live.

It has been possible that men would live.

It had been possible.

Over the edge of the cliff, up on to a new level, the creature there already, waiting, sprawling indolently, sucking a coppered wisp of grass. Sheep here on a new meadow – white woollen sheep – familiar sheep – yet sheep chewing intelligently. The light in the eye like a labrador – the look of cool assessment as you come over the edge of the cliff. They were being counted by sheep. Mycroft had to count back – twenty-five sheep. Berenice noted their stride, no mincing wobbling motion but a pin-stripe glide. They were sheep with intentions.

The coppered meadow inhabited by business sheep lay as peaceful in the morning as a college quad. Upon three sides they were surrounded by a white and stuccoed façade, a three-sided back drop, a surface studded in oblongs in rising graduated proportions with projections, a façade looking inwards and downwards at the arrivals. At intervals steps outwards, steps under the projections, steps leading up and out of the coppered quadrangle, out through the white sides – out where?

The creature watched them both but it did not move. It lay in the grass with buttons undone, soaking in the seeping warmth. One of the sheep walked boldly over to it, receiving a pat upon the head, a piece of sugar and a scratch, to return importantly and paid, back to its fellows in the centre of the lawn.

Mycroft felt impelled to walk across the square. (The sheep watched him. He felt himself to be an animal placed in a deliberate environment. But there was a difference. *He* knew that he had been placed here. Four right angles: three hundred and sixty degrees. To look back, the view over the lip of the cliff, down the meadowed stairs beneath the arching artificial trees, the view over the formal absurdity.

Beneath his feet the grass was burnished. Here the sheep were exploring – one digging industriously with a forefoot, three others looking carefully on and commenting.

Mycroft's hands moved over his suit, searching for what his mind looked for. Around him on three sides the white familiar façade, the oblongs, the projections supported by pillars, the sense of order, design and method – and from here to look out upon that world.

Berenice felt infected by the creature. She desired to go and sit on the grass and stretch. She sat, lay on the lawn floor of the quad and stretched in it, her pale hair on the grass, her thighs on the grass, her heels. Arch the back-bone. Stretch out the arms, the feet – they encompass the ground. And here, here if you did not look back, was a boundary to be contained by, an architectural space. Space and place, the business of living in architecture where one moved from one desired environment to an-other, where one arrived at a contained spot to receive a particular and constructed experience. To sit in the middle of a familiar Kensington square, or Islington square, or Bloomsbury square. Playing tennis with Bruce in Blooms-bury, Bruce in those shabby dogged flannels and his fear-some backhand shots, all the crude demented power of a blacksmith banging on his anvil.

Yet now the sheer excitement of opening her mind to a small quiet light – to the patient confidence. To accept where she was! Not to wish less than to see what she saw. To lie with one's body on the floor of the quad – then you clang like a bell.

She opened her eyes.

It nodded encouragingly.

Painlessly her wish was being . . .

'Not yet,' the creature teased. Its body stood over hers.

Mycroft could hear, in his mind's ear, Oona's feet hurrying down the steps under the high porchway (got your bag, dear?) even though the grass was here and their

Jaguar was not in sight beside the meter. He looked up at this high wall. On the top floor was his lab-room where Geoffrey liked to play, to send their private mice exploring down a new-made maze. This was number 34, the familiar number. Now there would be a different view from his room, a view back across the coppered grass and down the meadowed stairs. From up there one might begin a new notebook. Oona would be amused.

The creature coming over towards him, attracting him more than she should so that his hands wanted to walk over her.

But this level could be his table. It was as if . . .

The creature was smiling up at him, its shirt draped round its shoulders.

'Not yet,' it said.

16

Light, a precise illumination, a calculated vantage point. The creature in a crisp white coat, in charge.

Outside – nothing.

Within – careful preparation, two identical and elaborate chairs in stainless steel, a balanced clinical appearance but a designed comfort for those occupants paying attention, foot-rests, neck-rests, swivels. Each chair had its back turned round towards the other.

Each occupant has a supply of barley-sugars, a paper bag exactly folded, no cigarettes, a bottle of Vichy water and a crystal glass. Each swivel chair has a small table attached to the left arm-rest.

'Passengers will not make notes during the journey. The taking of photographs is strictly forbidden.'

The creature was in its element.

There was a tang of ether in the air.

Oona Charrington observed that they were now completely encircled by glass as if they were in some vast retort and they had to take the chair that was offered.

'Please be seated and kindly fasten your safety-belts. This seat here, Brother Nicholas. The belt is fastened – so.'

There was nothing to be seen through the brilliant sides of the retort – only light.

The creature was seated. It had a separate leather bucket seat. No switches, no dials, no controls, but the way it sat there you might have thought there were.

There was a sound, a note like a huge vacuum cleaner starting, but neither lurch nor vibration.

'Are we in a ship?' Brother Nicholas asked.

Oona decided that they were moving and then re-decided that it was an illusion.

Nothing moved.

The glass walls were dustless, stainless, sterile and hygienic. No outside influence, no object, no belonging, no sentiment to disturb the operation in progress. Only the precise whine of sound.

They had fastened their safety-belts. They could not unfasten them. They could not see each other.

'Nausea,' Oona reminded herself, 'can often be induced by a purely psychological disturbance.' She wondered how long it would be before she could get back to Mycroft. There was nothing to see, only light through the glass. She fumbled with the paper bag.

Disembodiment – floating, motion without a point of reference from which to draw conclusions.

The lights dimmed, slowly, almost imperceptibly.

'It's going dark,' Nicholas stated. Only then did he realize that he had stated it out loud. His hands sweated. The note, the whine, the howl of the machine was trying to the ears.

'Why doesn't it stop?' his voice spoke again. The glass

retort was both delving and rising into darkness. He felt a growing alarm at not being able to see – strapped in – the pitch of the whine screaming up and up into his ears. His feet squirmed on their foot-rest.

Oona sat waiting. It was not absolutely dark. She could make out her toes. There was a view now through the glass walls. It was the view that might have been expected: the lake from the house, the great arching columns and the stepped land beyond. Nothing was moving. They had not moved, yet there was an uneasy sense that they had turned round, that they were pointing in another direction, but there was no certainty. Also the colours – the place seemed slightly muted, as if seen through a tinted screen, a seeing through shades of grey.

'What is it all in aid of?' Oona found herself asking. The others made no reply. She could not see them even if she twisted her head, even if she leaned as far as the belt would allow. To drink water was something to do, water sparkling in a clear glass.

The machine continued.

The ground beneath them did begin to drop away. There was a void beneath their feet. Brother Nicholas was sucking a barley-sugar.

'You will wish to encourage the belief that you have travelled from one place to another,' the creature said in clear hostess terms.

Yet they paused. They were not rising any higher, they could see down again. Far over was a dazzling garden that they had not explored, a medley of pinks and blues, and for the first time they saw other houses set in coppered lawns with tiny figures moving among them.

No, it was not moving, they themselves were moving.

They had been down there and they had never visited all those places and now they were leaving.

There was darkness. The ceiling? Absolute darkness. The blooms, the golden tree-tops, they had gone from sight.

Nicholas realized with a start that he had not the faintest idea what they were travelling to. They just sat in their steel chairs and looked out at nothing. The note of their engine continued.

'The way up is faster than the way down,' the creature murmured.

Oona strained to look outwards, and also to remember the creature's words earlier. Absurd words. 'Whatever you shall want, you shall have.' She knew that she had no choice but to believe them. She had arranged the pattern of her thoughts like playing cards in her head. Up had come the temptations – the longing for rest and the greater longing for her own, their own, house. Mycroft sitting at his desk, making fun with his own diagrams, Geoffrey intent, shaping and trimming a length of balsa over a sheet of *The Times*. (Geoffrey must be with Mycroft now.) The next move in the game, the ear hearing the shrilling of the telephone and her hands would be lifting the mouthpiece and she would be talking about some real child in real trouble outside this home world that her eyes could see. Oona's eyes would watch Mycroft while she advised the house-man or calmed the elderly parent. 'Yes, she would come.' Here the necessity, the fascination, the duty, the betrayal of Mycroft sitting and enjoying her existence, back to the Jaguar, the sense of power under the foot, the lamplight gleaming on the wet streets as one hurried (it might not be necessary), the small girl with the unexpected haemorrhage, there were several possibilities, the brain watching the traffic, the jay-walkers crossing the reflections on the shining surface, change down, brake, and then away.

Sister Ingrid leading her to the bed, the child now sleeping (Geoffrey sleeping). Another pattern of cards in one's head – a trick won after careful contemplation of a poor hand. (We do not always get dealt a good hand.)

Mycroft always so patient with her endless disappearances. He still liked, enjoyed, washing her in the bath after a long day, he still enjoyed her existence and the warm soap and his hands over her shoulders, over herself. Her ears straining for the telephone. The grey-green tiles of the bathroom, they had chosen them for their relaxing qualities. Sister Ingrid was reliable, the feet in the hospital corridor at night.

Downstairs.

Downstairs under the trees she and Mycroft had gone walking. The unicorn had been grazing, delicate and unexpected blossoms had hung like wreaths across their path. They had walked barefoot on the moss high grass, going in no particular direction, enjoying the sensation of warmth and breathing, of saying nothing, strolling by the lake shore. That had been marvellously sufficient.

There was always a haunting dissatisfaction at not

being with Mycroft. Mycroft had been there since the beginning, all the patient way through her career. Yet he had always had more time during their marriage, time to think and write and be, while they had so enjoyed living with each other, the slight accusation at the back of her mind whenever they were parted. But also, the odd sense down there in the house beneath the trees, that they had been divorced from their careers. Yet it was enough to see Mycroft deftly making coffee, the drip of the black coffee.

The glass device, light not darkness forming beyond the transparent walls. The lack of enclosure: insecurity.

Oona Charrington was startled.

A grilled gate appeared to go vertically by, people standing beyond it, queuing and waiting, grey coats and grey faces. The gate descended, vanished below their feet. They were still rising. Darkness. A further grill floating down past them, a further crowd of waiting people, a further patch of darkness.

Oona felt the safety-belt release itself. Brother Nicholas was on his feet. The seats had gone. They had stopped rising. The next fate, the next moment, the next word on the page, what was to be written was to be written. What was certain was also to be known.

'South Kensington Station,' the voice said. 'You were both going to South Kensington. Now you have got there.'

And that, Brother Nicholas reflected, was not altogether true. I had done what I intended to do at South Kensington. I was coming away, I was leaving, and now I have

198

been brought back. What did Oona Charrington say, want: 'The old world, the place that is familiar, that we have always known.' This place was hardly familiar to him. South Kensington had itself been a mild adventure, a place where one must be cautious with the traffic, where people hurried without a framework, unhappily staring at what might be tomorrow, looking askance at his own measured pace. He had only asked to be allowed to go back and try. Try? Was it true that now South Kensington did not exist, that it had been destroyed, a mangled dustbowl? Or had they been put through a smooth experiment, would they merely be returned to where they had been, to feel themselves to be a kind of secret laughing-stock? Or a public one?

Does it matter if we are laughed at, if we are humiliated, if we are made fools – would not that be worth while if one could but see ... Brother John, Brother Bernard, Brother Geofric, Brother Frances, Brother Thomas, Brother Ulric, Brother Luc ...

The Prior listening once to his confession, his memories of his past, so often his past had lived with him, the days before Nicholas had entered this Order: a sailing dinghy running free before the wind, he had come down from Cambridge, successful with his degree and his misery, sailing with some friend's sister who had grown up suddenly, more familiar flesh in the sun. 'Even our temptations,' the Prior had said, 'are our treasures. Without them no right decision is ever possible. We must not fear what tempts us, we must fear even less the memory of what has tempted us. We must look at ourselves clearly and with sympathy and with understanding and while we firmly turn aside, we do not cast that memory and experience away from us. We keep it as a part of our life, our knowledge and our being. We even thank God, even for our failures, for this is our life that has been given to us, the very dimensions of this gift that has been granted to us and that we must value.'

Nicholas could remember their enjoyment as they looked out together across the sea from the monastery. He could remember that friend's sister, browner, more sweetly sly than even Astrid in the sun.

They stood together. The gates were opening. The hiss and the crash of metal. They opened out on to a passageway, the battered paintwork of London Transport.

'That way out, please.' A man in uniform directed them. Almost automatically they walked out. All together. The creature walked between them. It was South Kensington.

The clatter of coins tumbling. People giving coin and receiving cardboard. Insects about their rituals come unrecognized, perform their necessary act and then go down. People emerge, come up, have been transported.

I want to go back and try.

Nicholas remembered. Nicholas wondered.

How far back had he been taken?

Here was normality. Oona Charrington looked round. Normality washed round them like an incoming tide. People pushed by them. Here in South Kensington they were on ground level. They could look out across the roundabout. Buses in their tall overbearing scarlet forging through the dusty sunshine, taxis fussing like tugs. The house was only a few minutes away. She would ask Brother Nicholas . . .

They reached out for more normality. The coloured cars rolled by.

He would come.

Everything was as everything had been before. Nothing had happened. Oona had to telephone the hospital as soon as she got in. They had better have something. (Tea? What time was it? She did not seem to have her watch with her. Mycroft would not be along until later she supposed. Was there anything at home to offer?) She must write up her notes. Nothing was different.

The creature was still with them.

It had taken off the trim white coat. It was in bright green jeans, with a yellow shirt tied up in front and it walked between them. It seemed to know the way.

They crossed the roads, the roundabout. The crossings are particularly complex at South Kensington. Oona took in the movement of people, vehicles, and the back-cloth of wheeling shop-fronts, shops for the underclothes of women, for the bright new car shown under glass, for the place to drink coffee SARABIA, the illuminated instruction: CROSS NOW.

And they crossed.

A paper-seller: P.M. SPEAKS.

Brother Nicholas walked patiently. The creature took his hand across the road. Who was taking whom? (You will have time to go to Westminster, the creature said. The night train is not until 23.45 hours. The ticket and the seat-booking pressed into his hand. He had not planned to return to the mother house tonight. You have been recalled!)

It did not take them long to reach the square. The buildings were very white, very elegant, with rising graduated proportions. Oona confidently led the way to number 34.

No latchkey!

'Excuse me,' the creature said, smiling. It put its hand on the lock and the door was open.

They trooped inside. To Oona the house had only been left that morning – to see Geoffrey off. She made them sit down and bustled off towards the kitchen. Nicholas recognized the atmosphere of this huge living-room with Mycroft's desk in the window. He sat (sat without noticing, he noticed) in the comfortable chair. The creature sat cross-legged at his feet. The little monk was in a well-known strange place. The Persian carpet under his feet, the soft and surrounding swivelling chair upon which he sat, the easy presence of the serene enfolding room, these things were familiar foreign things. 'Now' was simply a pause, a limbo before he could, unbelievably, return to his community.

'I can return?' he asked the creature questioningly.

'You must return,' it insisted, tilting back its head to look at him, to smile at his half disbelief.

'In fact nothing has been destroyed,' Nicholas mused.

'Everything has been destroyed. Everything is destroyed. Everything is always destroyed. But you had a wish. You wished differently. I am granting your wishes. There are many roads. They always exist. You can only walk one of them. I know them all. I have put you on a different road. But the first road still continues and will always continue. Some of the roads are long, some short, and they have no end, but they all lead to the same place.'

Nicholas bowed his head. It would not let him be afraid. The creature was merciful, an endless mercy that would not let him remember.

'So I begin again,' he heard himself say. 'Not as I really expected – yet my wish has been . . .'

The creature held up a finger.

'Not yet,' it warned him.

There was the sound of teacups on a tray.

Oona had a feeling that there were more things in her refrigerator than when she had last seen it. The newspapers were – well they were this morning's papers, the ones they had had breakfast over. (Geoffrey had forgotten his cutting.) She had not lost any days. She had gained. She had telephoned the hospital and everything was in good order.

There was the creature drinking her tea, Nicholas refusing sugar. She should know by now that he did not take it in tea. Afterwards she had better go and check over Geoffrey's room and find out what else he had forgotten this term. There was usually something to send on. Of course, it being Wednesday, Mycroft would by now have gone on to his committee.

The creature was enjoying a slice of Swiss roll. It had

quite the rudest health Oona had ever observed. The skin glowed, the muscles were like steel springs. She knew the teeth were perfect (with their extra pair) while the shape and arrangement were a little different, the molars a little wider, the eye-teeth more sharp. It had only been after watching it for some time that Oona had noticed that its ears pricked under its hair. Not so acutely as a cat perhaps, but the creature's ears certainly turned towards sound. Its nostrils dilated, felt out towards the air. Under its arms the fur was black, but over its body, it was most notice-able if you ran your fingers over its backbone, there was a thick almost invisible down about the colour of its skin.

The door-bell rang.

'That's the dry-cleaning man,' Oona pronounced.

'I'll go,' the creature insisted. It even knew where the ticket was. It was running to the door. Mycroft's tweed suit! A huge jet rumbled overhead. Oona and Nicholas grimaced at each other. The sound of voices – and the creature came triumphantly back. (One would suppose that its supply of currency would be endless.)

'Just lay it on the chair, dear.' Oona sipped her tea.

'You *have* granted me my . . .' she began to admit.

'You don't know all the things you may have wished,' the creature said softly. 'Not yet, but when you have finished your tea, then go and look out of the window.'

Oona and Brother Nicholas drank down their tea. The creature stood by them, small, alert, standing first on one leg and then on the other.

Almost imperceptibly the room had filled with a yellow

and artificial light. Somewhere a car horn blared, but very far away.

Nicholas had his back to the window while he drank. Already Oona had twitched the curtain. The monk put down his cup and turned about.

Across the square the coppered pasture was thick and lush and the sheep banqueted, conversing and circulating like well-lined stockbrokers at an earnest cocktail party. Far away the arching artificial landscape was leading down, level by level, like a gigantic stairway to the green lake so many miles still below. Suspended under a neighbouring porchway a blood-red snouted bat hung, big as a pony and upside-down, stretching a pillar-box wing with idle luxury. Mycroft watched it as he watched his wife and the monk standing at the window, looking out towards him, looking out from his house. Berenice had not noticed. She was drawing a small white bear who had importuned, who had demanded and was now posing importantly in front of her. Far away the unicorn were moving again, horns held high.

Mycroft and Oona waved to each other.

'The view in and the view out – you will never escape them,' the creature explained. 'They are both still there, even when you shut your eyes.'

Mycroft was hardly listening. In a quiet way he was relieved to see Oona. (Cup of tea, dear?) He had remembered his door-key. There was nothing very peculiar about stepping from one world to the other. One could go on doing it. He even tried it. Forward and back, forward and back. The lavender touch of Oona's polish – the spiced air of the other place. He could walk back and look at the bat. It opened one eye and looked at him. He could walk into his own hall and find his slippers, where Oona always tidied them. He glanced out of the open front door.

Berenice heard the creature coming up behind her. The bear waved an off-hand paw. The creature blew a raspberry. Berenice carried on working, her fingers smudged with charcoal. She had even got it on her knees. She must draw big. The creature whispered in Berenice's ear.

'I shall come in a little while,' Berenice replied. 'Maybe when I've finished this.' (People were never satisfied. They always wanted you to move on just when you had reached the thing that mattered. It was staying, not moving, that was important.)

'She is the easiest to satisfy,' the creature was explaining over a second round of tea when Brother Nicholas was trying to say good-bye. 'She doesn't need to come back often. In a way she has always been there. Off to Westminster?'

Nicholas nodded. He had found a place to put his tea-cup down. The yellow artificial light still shone into the room. The little white bear was being introduced to lumps of sugar.

'I think I know why I am wanted back tonight – so quickly.'

He looked at the creature, not hoping to hear hope, but simply to hear.

'A new Prior has to be chosen,' it said. 'For him the bomb fell. The bomb falls for all of you, one by one and in due season. It has always fallen. It fell before it was invented. It does not fall on me. For each of you and in due season I will open my hand and it will fall.'

The monk bowed his head.

'Kiss me,' the creature commanded. 'No one can ever say good-bye to me. You can only kiss me.'

It stood, its arms akimbo, its feet turned slightly apart, carved hands, carved feet.

He kissed, and it was not only Astrid, bitter and sweet, forgiven and loved, but those many mornings when he had driven his tractor fieldward with the sun, a big red sun, lifting its head over the sea's horizon, or the voices of the brothers intoning the endless word, the belief and the mercy. Now there must be a new mercy.

The creature saw him off and in peace on his way to Westminster, a small figure in a brown habit striding past concrete.

Berenice had managed to lure the bear out again.

'Where's Geoff?' Mycroft was asking.

'I thought he was with you,' Oona said. (Had she?)

They suddenly looked aghast. They had not noticed his absence. Then Mycroft's face cleared. 'Why, of course, we saw him off to school yesterday, today, earlier.' He remembered the train, the faces at the window, the lean-faced diesel engine waiting to pull.

'He's not at school.' The creature was sitting on the end of their settee, swinging its legs.

'What do you mean, he's not at school?' Oona asked indignantly.

'I kidnapped him,' the creature replied, and its voice was rising. 'I told you. He told you. He is still downstairs. He is happy. No. Do not try to get him back. If you brought him across the doorway he would crumble, crumble into dust. Stay where you are. Please, you have something else to do. Something even more important. Please, you will have to keep me, look after me, give me some affection, help, loyalty, correction, support, encouragement. You will have to get me over school and when I have my moods you will understand and my enthusiasms will amuse you and when I refuse to marry him you will be glad to stand by me – because I too must be loved, I too want kindness and care and cheer and a welcome, though I bear all the weight of the world and the turn of the stars through all the blankness of time.'

And it was sobbing, sobbing on the floor at their feet and Mycroft bent down and lifted it up and put it on his knee and Oona took hold of its hands and smoothed back the dark hair from its face and it was theirs and South Kensington looked through their window.